978-1913-3160-37

AF085893

U.K.
RAVE FLYERS

1991 - 1996

For Stefania Fiorendi and Junior Tomlin

NOW Every Sat   **10pm - 8am**
ALL NIGHTER
AT THE EMPIRE, MARINE RD, MORECAMBE, LANCS.

Presenting:

PAUL WALKER - ROB TISSERA - MATT BELL- PAUL TAYLOR - JOHN J - WAYNE ESSENTIAL
Plus special guest D.J's

| SAT 4th Sept: MARK GREEN | SAT 11th Sept: MIKE E-BLOC | SAT 18th Sept: CHRIS BAKER | SAT 25th Sept: MALC |

UPFRONT GOING FROM STRENGTH TO STRENGTH. BRING YOU LIVE ON STAGE:
BASSRATE (RHYTHM NATION) - P.A. SAT 11th SEPT

MORE GUEST D.J.'s - BIGGER PRODUCTION & LIGHTING SHOW - LASERS -
VIRTUAL REALITY - VIDEO PROJECTION & GRAPHICS - BOUNCY CASTLE -
GAMES ROOM - GYROSCOPE. FULLY LICENSED BAR TILL 2AM + FRUIT & JUICE BAR

M.Y.L SECURITY (Tight but polite)   **ADM £10**

INFO & COACH LINE 0524 62531

MEMBERSHIP APPLICATION FORM   I am 18 years or over,
please send me membership for UP FRONT PROMOTIONS.

NAME ....

ADDRESS ....

POST CODE .... DATE OF BIRTH ....

CARLISLE

MORECAMBE   BLACKBURN

LANCASTER

FLEETWOOD   LEEDS

BLACKPOOL   PRESTON

LIVERPOOL   MANCHESTER

ONLY 1 HOUR FROM
Manchester-Leeds-Carlisle-Liverpool

DIRECTIONS
from Junction 34 of M6 Follow
signs for Morecambe &
Frontierland & this will take you
right to our front main entrance
on the promenade.

CHESHIRE PRINT & DESIGN 061 477 5771   0831 810 969

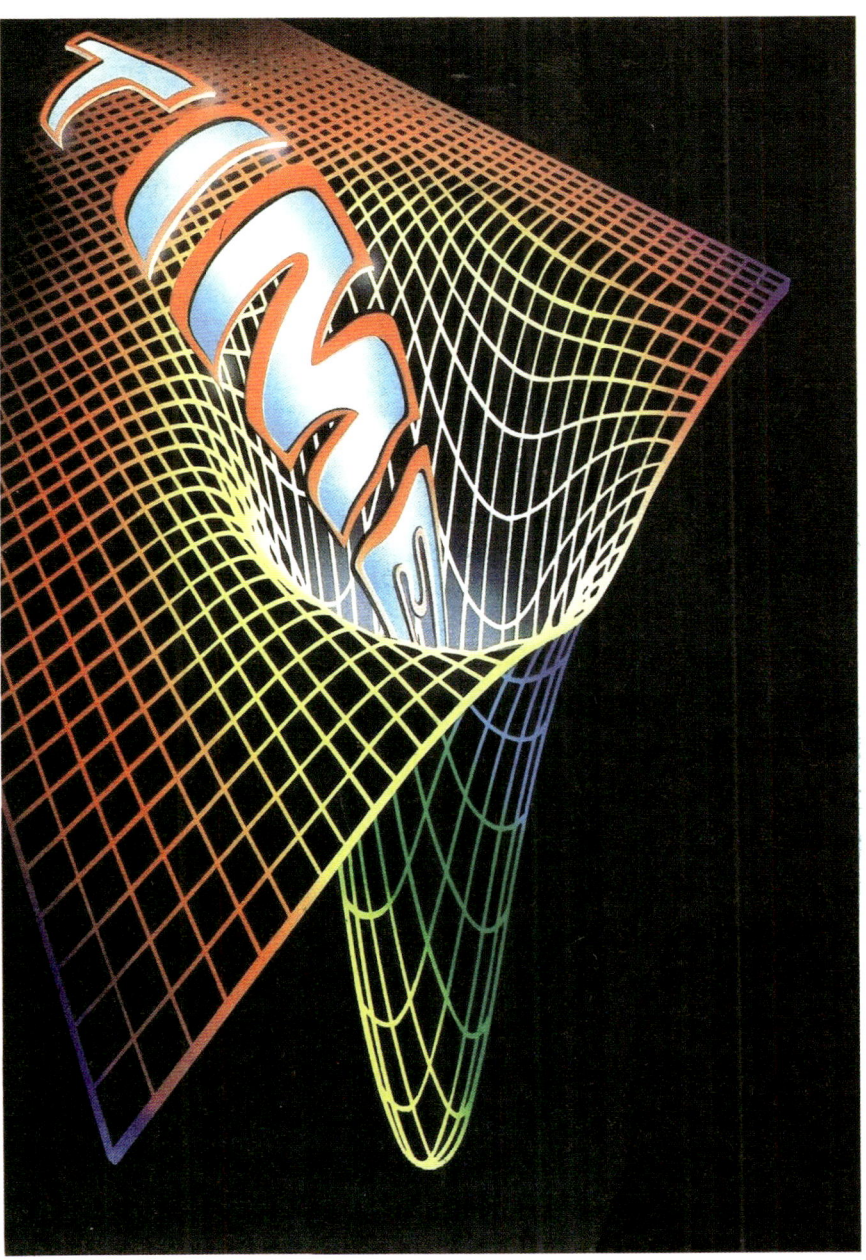

The Time® Organization proudly present

PART TWO
INTO THE FUTURE?

ALL NIGHT: FRIDAY 19TH APRIL, 1991
AT THE ASTON VILLA SPORTS & LEISURE CENTRE
8 ASTON HALL ROAD BIRMINGHAM B6 7LB
START:8.30PM   FINISH: 7AM

FABIO GROOVERIDER **SASHA**
MICKY FINN KEITH SUCKLING
EASY GROOVE SIMON SMITH

PERFORMING LIVE ON STAGE SHADES OF RHYTHM
Taking you through Time®: **MC MASTER P**

After the overwhelming success of New Years Eve, which was the largest legal
Warehouse party in the Midlands, the Time® Organization are proud to present
another all nighter at Birminghams largest indoor venue, Aston Villa Leisure
Centre. This event is going to be tops with a spectacular vari-light show
also 3d holographic 7 colour laser. Very loud sound. Also, Human Gyroscope.
Beautiful Decorations and visuals. GlitterBombs. Dance Risers. Live on stage.
The Time® Dancing Machine. (this event is not to be missed)

TICKETS £18 (PLUS BOOKING FEE)
CREDIT CARD HOTLINE: 021 328 5377

TICKET OUTLETS

Bath • Soul Survival 0225 448744 **Birmingham** • Aston Villa Leisure Centre Box Office 021 328 5377 **Birmingham** • The Depot 021 643 6045 **Bristol** • Replay Records 0272 265954 **Bristol** • Tonys Records 0272 214659 **Cambridge** • Chauvenist 0223 321372 **Coventry** • Revive Clothing 0203 550750 **Cheltenham** • Selina. BadLands 0242 227725 **Daventry** • A D Bates 0327 77731 **Derby** • BPM Records 0332 382038 Way Ahead 0332 361371 **Gloucester** • Ruthless Records 0452 309960 **Hanley** • Mike Loyd 0782 214641 **Leeds** • Crash Records 0532 436743 **Leicester** • Westwood Clothing 0533 519128 **Liverpool** • Three Beat Records 051 709 3355 **London** • Black Market Records 071 437 0478 **London** • Mash/Passion Records 071 434 9609 **Luton** • Soul Sense 0582 2337 **Manchester** • Piccadilly Box Office 061 839 0858 **Newport** • Diverse Music 0633 259661 **Northampton** • Spin A Disc 0604 31144 **Norwich** • Backs Records 0603 625658 **Nottingham** • Just Groove Records 0602 475008 Way Ahead 0602 414212 **Oxford** • Manic Hedgehog Records 0865 246069 **Peterborough** • Steve Jason Ticket Agency 0733 60075 **Sheffield** • Warp Records 0742 757585 **Walsall** • Zoot 0922 771186 **Wolverhampton** • Ruby Red 0902 771186

TICKET AGENTS

Brighton • Richard 0903 208031 or 0860 44416 **Leicester** • Stuart 0860 805021 **Grimsby** • Mick 0472 356601 **Oxford** • Zina 0831 577474 **Stoke** • Pete 0831 448808 **Telford** • Errol 0952 200761 **London** • East London-Warren 0836 799072 North London-Jeremy 0860 650661 **Portsmouth** • Darren 0860 214421 **Swindon** • Nick 0793 525755 **West Midlands** • Jonno 0860 921116

INFORMATION DETAILS 0898 866333
Please note the date of this event has been changed from
Saturday 13th April as advertised last time.

Urgent enquiries Time® Organisation 021 454 2967

BIRMINGHAM'S RAG MARKET

11.00PM SUNDAY 5TH MAY 1991
ALL NIGHT UNTIL
12.00AM (MIDDAY) BANK HOLIDAY MONDAY 6TH MAY 1991

IN THE HEART OF BIRMINGHAM, ENGLAND'S SECOND CITY, LIES AN ENORMOUS BRICK BUILT WAREHOUSE(THE BIRMINGHAM RAG MARKET), IT IS GEOGRAPHICALLY THE CENTRE OF THE COUNTRY

ON
SUNDAY 5th MAY 1991 AT 11.00pm.

RUNNING THROUGH ALL NIGHT UNTIL '2.00AM MIDDAY BANK HOLIDAY MONDAY

THIS VENUE WILL BE TRANSFORMED BY TWO OF THE NORTHS TOP DANCE ORGANIZATIONS TO HOLD THE BIGGEST ALL NIGHT DANCE EVENT

WE BRING TOGETHER THE COUNTRY'S **TOP D.J.'S**, **LIVE ACTS** AND **GENUINE ATTRACTIONS** IN ONE VENUE. INSIDE A MASSIVE **80, 000 SQ FT WAREHOUSE** RUNNING THROUGH **ALL NIGHT UNTIL 12.00 MIDDAY** BANK HOLIDAY MONDAY

This is the event of the year (We guarantee) Not to be missed
TOGETHER THE COUNTRY WILL DANCE IN HARMONY

GENERAL INFORMATION : 0898 866333 (44p peak, 33p off peak)
Tickets and other information : 0836 556389 / 0836 556319

UNDERGROUND PROMOTIONS & THE TIME ORGANIZATION
PRESENT
Together 91

11.00pm Sunday 5th May 1991 *All Night Until* **12.00 am Midday Bank Holiday Monday, Birmingham's Rag Market**

A Whole new concept of entertainment waiting to be explored, For 12 Hours you will Witness

ATTRACTIONS,

☆ 80 000sq ft Of Pure Dance Arena,
☆ Three Amazing Multicolour 3D Holographic Computer Aided Laser Display Systems - An original production of human intelligence (Showing for the first time ever - Mind Bending Laser Battle),
☆ High Tech Graphically controlled Visual Effects & Lighting.
☆ Space Simulator, Gyroscopes, Bronco Billy & a whole new concept of pleasure rides.
☆ 30,000sq ft of outdoor stalls, sideshows & attractions,
☆ 65K of ultimate sound system (Genuine),
☆ Dancers , Clowns, Inflatables, Jugglers, Illuminous Face, Body Paint Stalls,
☆ Live T.V. Screens, Fresh Fruit Stalls, Photographers, Full Food Refreshments.

D.J's ON THE NIGHT

		EASY GROOVE	BRISTOL
KEITH SUCKLING	BIRMINGHAM	ANDY CAROL	LIVERPOOL
CARL COX	BRIGHTON	D.J. RAP	LONDON
FABIO	LONDON	SIMON SMITH	DERBY
SASHA	MANCHESTER	GROOVE RIDER	LONDON
MICKY FINN	LONDON	DOC SCOTT	COVENTRY

LIVE P.A.TO BE ANNOUNCED

M.C. LENNY . M.C. HARDCORE GENERAL & M.C. MAN PARRIS

THERE IS NO OTHER EVENT HAPPENING ON THIS NIGHT
THIS EVENT HAS A FULL ENTERTAINMENT LICENCE

YOU WILL NOT BE DISAPPOINTED

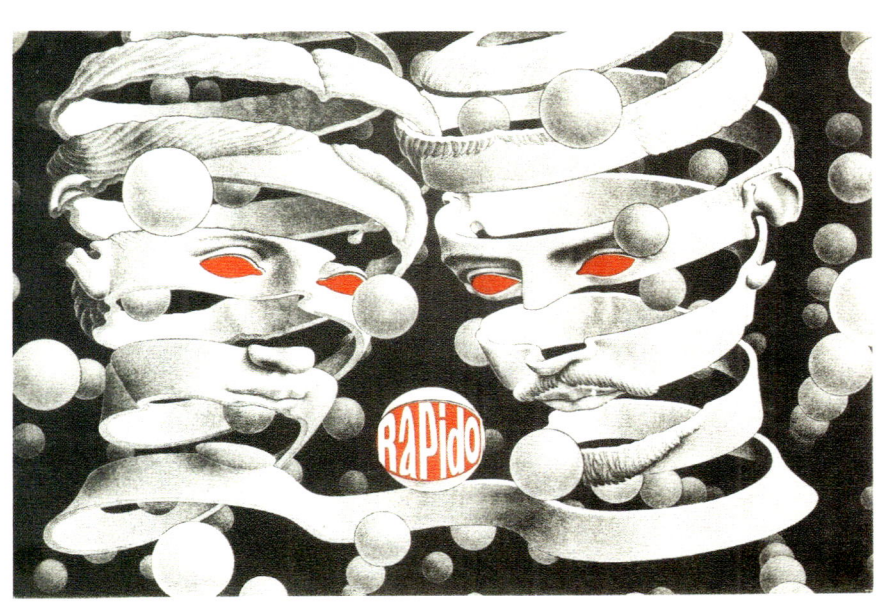

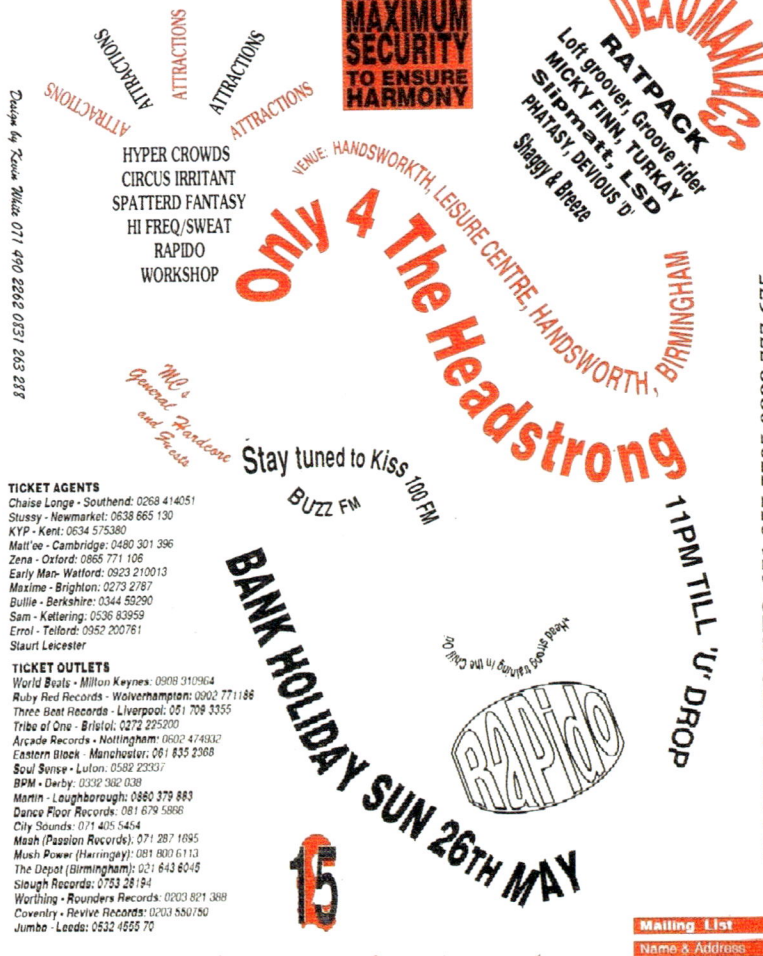

Design by Xenia White 071 490 2202 0131 263 288

ATTRACTIONS ATTRACTIONS ATTRACTIONS ATTRACTIONS ATTRACTIONS

WE PROMISE MAXIMUM SECURITY TO ENSURE HARMONY

DEXOMANIACS

RATPACK
Loft groover, Groove rider
MICKY FINN, TURKAY
Slipmatt, LSD
PHATASY, DEVIOUS 'D'
Shaggy & Breeze

HYPER CROWDS
CIRCUS IRRITANT
SPATTERD FANTASY
HI FREQ/SWEAT
RAPIDO
WORKSHOP

VENUE: HANDSWORTH, LEISURE CENTRE, HANDSWORTH, BIRMINGHAM

Only 4 The Headstrong

11PM TILL 'U' DROP

MC's General Hardcore and Jungle

Stay tuned to Kiss 100 FM

BUZZ FM

COACHES & INFO LINES: 071-357 7705 0898 777 675

TICKET AGENTS
Chaise Longe - Southend: 0268 414051
Stussy - Newmarket: 0638 665 130
KYP - Kent: 0634 575380
Matt'ee - Cambridge: 0480 301 396
Zena - Oxford: 0865 771 106
Early Man- Watford: 0923 210013
Maxime - Brighton: 0273 2787
Bullie - Berkshire: 0344 59290
Sam - Kettering: 0536 83959
Errol - Telford: 0952 200761
Staurt Leicester

TICKET OUTLETS
World Beats - Milton Keynes: 0908 310964
Ruby Red Records - Wolverhampton: 0902 771186
Three Beat Records - Liverpool: 051 709 3355
Tribe of One - Bristol: 0272 225200
Arcade Records - Nottingham: 0602 474932
Eastern Block - Manchester: 061 835 2388
Soul Sense - Luton: 0582 23337
BPM - Derby: 0332 382 038
Martin - Loughborough: 0860 379 883
Dance Floor Records: 081 679 5866
City Sounds: 071 405 5454
Mash (Passion Records): 071 287 1695
Mush Power (Harringey): 081 800 6113
The Depot (Birmingham): 021 643 6045
Slough Records: 0753 28194
Worthing - Rounders Records: 0203 821 388
Coventry - Revive Records: 0203 550750
Jumbo - Leeds: 0532 4555 70

BANK HOLIDAY SUN 26TH MAY

Headstrong Training in the Cool O.

RAPIDO

15

Mailing List
Name & Address
Birthday Telephone
write out and
return to unit C
Cromwell House
London SE1 9HP

Rapido is bringing its own brand of rave to the Midlands and promises to Rock the Socks off any Hardcore - Headstrong raver.
Tickets are destined to move fast. get on the case or listen out 4 the story!

EASTER THURSDAY
16th APRIL 1992   10pm til LATE
ON STAGE:
TOXIC 2

SPECIAL GUEST DJ: MOBY

MAIN DISCO	DJ's UPSTAIRS	MEMBERS BAR
Dominic	Trevor Fung	Robert Fung
Fabio	Colin Faver	Grant Harper
Grooverider	Steve Johnson	

THE WHITE PARTY

RAGE

Entrance: Members £6 All Night   Members Guests: £10 All Night
Over 18 Years Only.   Management Reserve the Right to Refuse Admission

~OBSESSION~

ESTABLISHED 1989 PRESENT

Passion Passion Passion

at
THE SANCTUARY
DENBEIGH LEISURE COMPLEX,
V7 SAXON STREET,
BLETCHLEY,
MILTON KEYNES
(Map on Ticket)

HAVE YOU GOT
THE KNOWLEDGE?

on
FRIDAY THE 2ND
OF APRIL
NINETEEN HUNDRED
AND NINETY THREE
ALL NIGHT EVENT

9PM UNTIL 7AM

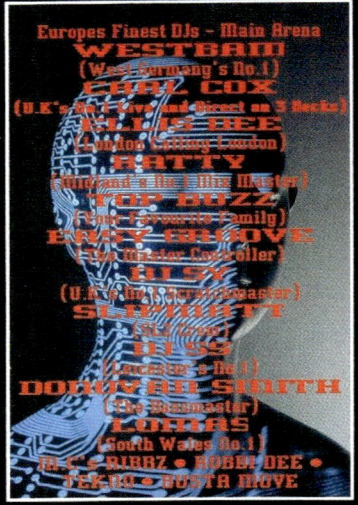

Europes Finest DJs – Main Arena
WESTBAM
(West Germany's No.1)
CARL COX
(U.K's No.1 Live and Direct on 3 Decks)
ELLIS DEE
(London / Ellis / London)
RATTY
(Midland's No.1 Mix Master)
TOP BUZZ
(Time Forward Family)
EASY GROOVE
(The Master Controller)
DLSX
(U.K's No.1 Scratchmaster)
SLIPMATT
TOP BUZZ
DJ SS
(Leicester's No.1)
DOUGAL & SMITH
(The Bassmaster)
LOMAS
(South Wales No.1)
MC's RIBBZ ● ROBBIE DEE ●
TEK NO ● DOUTA MOVE

After the success of Obsession's previous exploits-
Notably Peace Fest 2, 3RD Dimension (Largest ever
crowd at Westpoint), Passion – New Years Day –to
name but a few – The U.K's leading organisers of Dance
Events proudly present Passion. The U.K's most
futuristic purpose built indoor (and we mean indoor)
dance venue - The Sanctuary - will host this
unforgettable evening of House, Techno and Trance.
SOUND OF THE OBSESSION – ALWAYS ONE STEP AHEAD ~

LIVE P.A. FROM CRIMINAL MINDS
(CAN'T BEAT THE SYSTEM - GO WITH THE FLOW)

Progessive House Zone
Arena Two

JOHN KELLY
(Liverpool / Hacienda)
DJ ICE
(Norway's No.1)
DJ JACK (DIY)
(Top Free Party DJ)
JACK SMOOTH
(London's Top Remixer)

MIKE C
(Hacienda)
THE BANDIT
(New Talent)
DJ D.S.
(South Wales)
DJ A.N.D
(New Talent)

ATTRACTIONZ • EUROPE'S proven No.1 DJs in 2 (TWO) Dance Arenas • TWO 15' x 20' Interplanetary Projection Screens • 50K (FIFTY) of Crystal Clear Renegade Sound (as Featured at Peace Fest 2) • Rubber Clad Erotik Dancers strapped in 4 Giant Steel cages • Creative Backdrops by Banneranza • Our Usual Superior lighting display to expand your visual horizons • Unique hydraulic scissor lift for DJ platform • TWO full spectrum lasers parting the heavens with a matrix of 3D hologralik images • Visual Unique friendly Atmosphere • Laser Android • Security Video monitored FREE - and we mean FREE • Car Parking • James and his Giant Peach • Kelusw Obsession Gear by Daniel Poole • Special Purpose built 3D stage by Star Systems London • Professional Polite but Firm security by Specialised for absolute peace of mind • Stringent (but Fair) searches on entry • Klean (CLEAN) wash rooms • Strictly Over 18 • Don't waste your time trying to forge our new tickets R.O.A.R. We reserve the right to be selective - This will be an attitude and stress free area. Discs on sale 24th Feb. INFO. LINE 0242 255058. Flyer Concept & Design AFN Grafix 0242 255 058

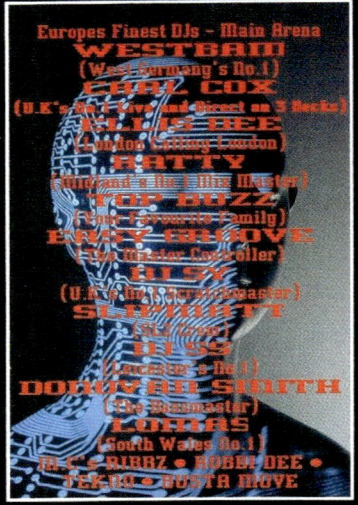

ADVANCE TICKET PRICE £16.50 + BOOKING FEE (WHERE APPLICABLE)- MORE ON DOOR - IF AVAILABLE
WITH ALL PREVIOUS EVENTS SELLING OUT IN ADVANCE, WE STRONGLY ADVISE EARLY TICKET PURCHASE TO ENSURE ENTRY.

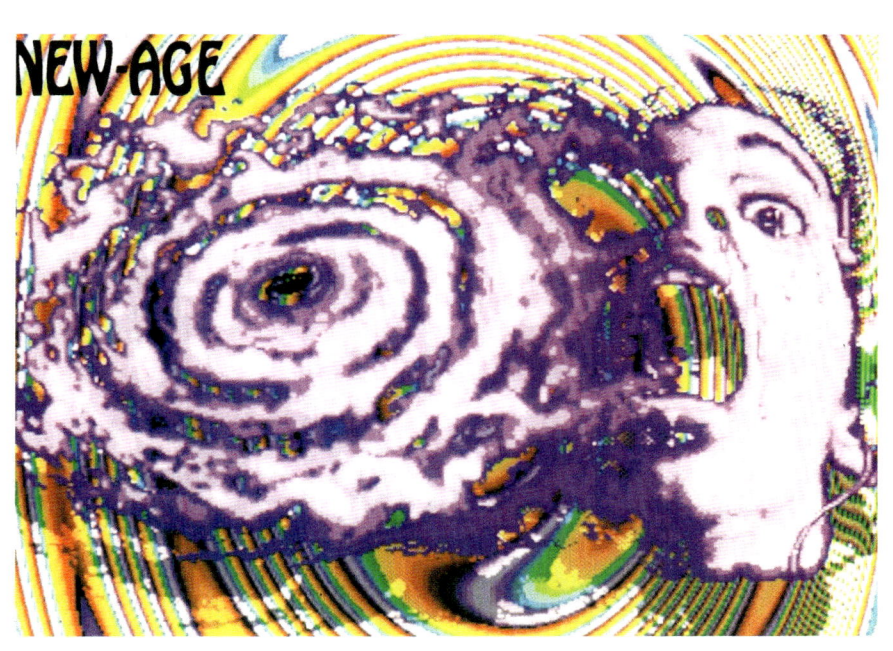

£15
MORE
AT
DOOR
+ maximum £1
Booking Fee

FRIDAY 24th JANUARY 1992

NEW-AGE

present

TICKET OUTLETS

Ticket Info 0203 559075
Event Info 0839 654294

NEW YEAR ... NEW AGE

30K SOUND

at
The
ECLIPSE
LOWER FORD STREET, COVENTRY

10 pm to 8 am

PREPARE YOURSELF FOR ANOTHER NEW-AGE SPECTACULAR

AFTER OUR CHRISTMAS ECSTASY, WE STRONGLY ADVISE EARLY TICKET BUYING
GUARANTEED MADNESS — GUARANTEED SELL-OUT — FOR THOSE IN THE KNOW!

UPSTAIRS					DOWNSTAIRS				
FABIO	**STU ALLAN**	**DJ SEDUCTION** 3 Dexs	**GROOVE RIDER**	**MICKY FINN**	**CARL WILLIAMS**	**NEIL TRIX**	**MICKY PARKS**	**MICKY WILSON**	**DR H**
SOUTH	Piccadilly Key 1.03	SOUTH	SOUTH	SOUTH	MIDLANDS	MIDLANDS	MIDLANDS	MIDLANDS	MIDLANDS

ATTRACTIONS:
NICE BIG INFLATABLES · ROBOTS · 7 COLOURED LASERS · UNICYCLIST · BACKDROPS · BALLOONS · YOU

NEW-AGE — PURE VALUE FOR MONEY

NEW-AGE
BACK AGAIN !

ALL NIGHT, FRIDAY 13th SEPTEMBER 9 pm - 8 am
AS USUAL BE EARLY PEOPLE — GET YOUR MONEY'S WORTH

NEW-AGE

PROMOTIONS

presents

HITE - NITE IV

at

The ECLIPSE
LOWER FORD STREET, COVENTRY

FRIDAY, 13th SEPTEMBER

All or our 3 events so far have been sell-outs, so please be early — our line-up agains shows that NEW-AGE know what you want

WE ARE SPENDING MORE AGAIN TO BRING YOU THE BEST ENTERTAINMENT MONEY CAN BUY

25K of TURBO SOUND

CHECK LINE UP

ALL 3 FLOORS KICKIN'

CHECK LINE UP

TOP DJs ON ALL FLOORS

TOP FLOOR DJs

TOP BUZZ	GROOVE RIDER	CARL COX	SLIPMATT	LUKE

2nd FLOOR

CARL WILLIAMS :: NEIL TRICK :: D.J. STEPH

MC ON THE NIGHT: **MAN PARRIS**

£15

TICKET More at Door

ATTRACTIONS:
GOLDENSCANS, FLOWER STROBES, UNICYCLIST, BALLOONS, INDOOR BOMBS, SEVEN COLOUR LASERS, BACKDROPS BY LETTUCE, FREEBIES AS USUAL, WHISTLES, FOG HORNS

£15

TICKET More at Door

INFO LINE: 0898-777675
Tickets on sale from Moonshine Records, opp. The Eclipse from Wednesday, September 11.

THE MAGNIFICENT SEVEN RAVE AGAIN

RAVE-IVAL...THE BIG ONE...
SUMMER HAS ARRIVED...IT'S TIME.

THE BIGGEST ALNIGHT PARTY SINCE 1989.

Date...25/26 May 1991...start...25 (10p.m.) — 26 May (noon).

Since the 80's a massive party has not taken place until now. It's time to re-emerge. 'cause this will not be your normal couple of thousand hold venue, this will be massive. A 20,000 capacity venue. The indoor venue is twice the size of the sunrise air hangar, a complete full scale funfare situated just outside the venue. This is just the beginning and the first of the summer festivals. Not since the day's of biology, sunrise and energy have we seen mass hysteria of thousand's of car's packed on motorway's. It's time to turn back the clock. **HYSTERIA IS BACK.**

NIRVANA...HYSTERIA...ENIGMA...STORM THE BASS
(London)   (Manchester)   (London)   (Bristol)

THE FOLLOWING...LIVE...RAW & CHAOS
(Yorkshire)   (London)   (Midlands)

———————THE MAGNIFICENT SEVEN RAVE AGAIN ———————

ATTRACTION

(due to the early flyer all act's are in the process of being confirmed)

Steve Jackson, Jason Jay, Stevie B, Mike Pickering, Judge Jule's. (LIVE) Lisa 'm' (rock to the beat) (move your body) (LIVE) A J&T C (mix 'n' play).

Confirmed
Carl Cox (Brighton) Groove Rider (London) Eddie Richards (London) P

Couzins (Portsmouth) Betts & Brisk (Hants) Ty Holden (London) Aubrey (Portsmouth) The Colonel (London) Cutmaster G (London) KU (London) Mr. C (London) Stevie H (Manchester) M.C. Smash (Blackburn) Mr. Hyde (Stevie Hi (Southampton)

Live
Urban Hype (Evar) J.D. (Dover) Sweet Sensation Krush (Let's Dance) Enzo (London) Hardcore Uproar (Blackburn)

TICKET AND INFO LINE'S OPEN From THE '22nd May 1991'

Rose (London) 071-2672607
Carrie (Bournemouth) 0202 769254
Simon (Birmingham) 0860 729214
Darren (Hants) 0860 214421
Steve (E. London) 0860 877358
Craig (W. London) 0860 869214 After 6pm
Jeremy (N. London) 0860 650661
Gary (N. London) 0831 578135
Martin (S. London) 0831 378555
Maxine (Brighton) 0273 27857
KYP (Kent) 0634 575380
Simon (London) 0836 557989
Anton (Blackburn) 0831 228853
Lee (London) 0831 620970
Julie (Portsmouth) 0705 261815
Craig (Nth London) 0992 769763
Dave (Nth London, Enfield) 0992 763783
Angie (Portsmouth) 0705 269628

Gary (Portsmouth) 0831 810661
Soul Survival (Bath) 0225 448744
Replay Records (Bristol) 0272 265954
X Records (Boston) 0204 391459
World Class (Colchester) 0206 768979
Revive Clothing (Coventry) 0203 550750
Premadonna Records (Cambridge) 0223 314365
Ruthless Records (Gloucester) 0452 309960
Mark (Guildford) 0831 242017
Chris (Hertfordshire) 0831 430495
Selina (High Wycombe) 0494 444250
Duncan (Hull) 0482 802410
Jumbo Records (Leeds) 0532 455570
3 Beat Records (Liverpool) 051 7093355
Andy (Maidstone) 0622 741452
Spur inn (Manchester) 061 8344483
Jason (Manchester) 061 3700984
Keith (Milton Keynes) 0908 609767

Neil (Newcastle) 091 4 32899
Simon (Northampton) 0536 713605
Backs Records (Norwich) 0603 629658
Zena (Oxford) 0831 577474
Manic Hedgehog Records (Oxford) 0865 246069
The Music Box (Plymouth) 0705 872877
Carole (Shrewsbury) 0743 791472
The Retreat (Stroud) 0453 750208
Pete (Stoke) 0831 448808
Revival Records (Swindon) 0793 542093
Errol (Telford) 0952 200761
Paul (Torquay) 0803 324116
Becky (Watford) 0923 229276
Jonno (West Midlands) 0860 921116
Dexy (South Midlands) 0386 40539
Ruby Red Records (Wolverhampton) 0902 771186
Red Rhino Records (York) 0904 636499

AS we know the rave scene is beginning to explode from the underground scene back into the open, here in London (rave-on) especially & also as far afield as Leed's, Wale's, Nottingham, Birmingham, Portsmouth, Coventry, Cambridge, Liverpool, Manchester, Bournemouth, Bristol and even as far as Scotland. WE hear you, we cut the limit it's time to join us as one and kick ass.

———————MEETING POINTS...10p.m. - 11p.m. ———————

WATFORD GAP (M1) (north)...SOUTH MIMMS (M25)...Astoria
Brixton (outside fridge)...Shepherds Bush (outside Mcdonalds)
Kings Cross (central)...Dungeons (east)

**60k rig, huge lazer show, 4 decks, one floor,
tickets £15.00 (old prices) in advance, venue will not be postponed.**

STORM THE BASS

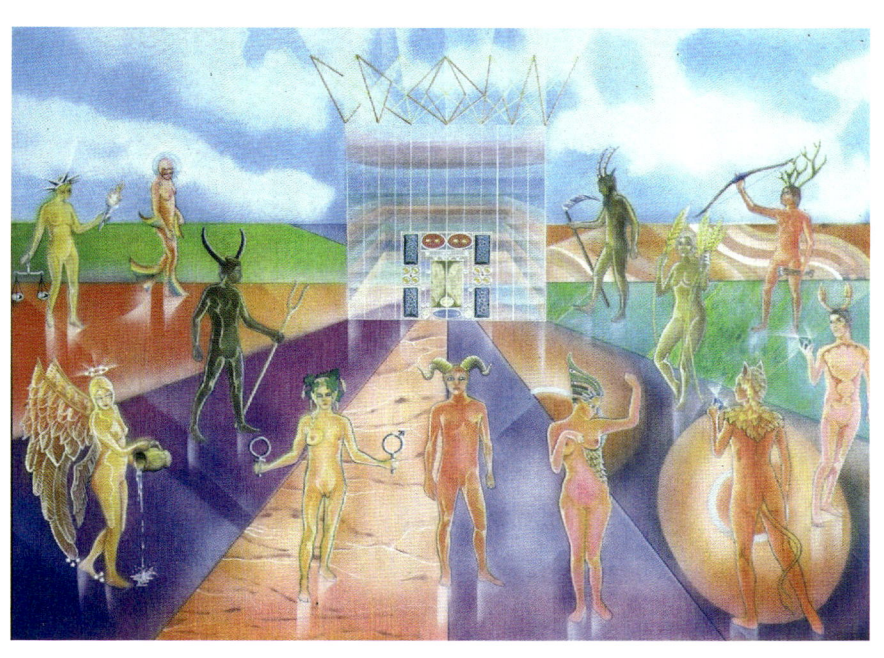

The Pirate Club

PRESENTS

FUTURE MYTH

SATURDAY 4TH DECEMBER 1993

AT

THE ROLLER EXPRESS

LEA VALLEY ESTATE, EDMONTON, LONDON N18

£11 IN ADVANCE 10pm to 6 am

£11 IN ADVANCE 10pm to 6 am

VINYL MYSTICS

SLIPMATT ✦ RANDALL ✦ ELLIS DEE ✦ DJ RAP
HIGHLANDER ✦ MIX MASTER MAX

ATLANTIS

GRAHAM GOLD ✦ ROBBIE CHARLES ✦ MEDZ ✦ BONES

ATTRACTIONS

40K Pirate Sound System - The Latest and Greatest Intelligent Lights and FX - Lasers - 7 Watts of Pure Light - 5 Massive Video Screens, with Roller Archive Footage and Live Edits on the night - Full Atmosphere plus our usual Attractions - Brain Machines - Face Painting - Video Arcade - Psyco Active Food Bar - Champagne bar - Secure Parking - Polite Security - Cloakroom - Personal Lockers - Plus Much More!
STOP PRESS: LIMITED EDITION PIRATE CLUB JACKETS MA1 OR MA2 £49

CREDIT CARD HOTLINE 24hr (081) 807 7345 INFORMATION HOTLINE 24hr (081) 887 0357

TICKET OUTLETS

LONDON			KENT		
Archway	Pure Groove	071 281 4877	Ashford	Richard Records	0233 629 706
Bethnal Green	Total Music	071 473 3000	Chatham	Loco	0634 818 330
Bromley	Bluebird	081 313 3413	Gravesend	Biting Back	0474 321 931
Camden	Zoom	071 267 4479	Herne Bay	White Label	0227 742 691
Central	Unity	071 734 2746	Kent	(Mobile Delivery)Paul	0860 494 527
Chelsea	Lucky Spin	071 351 6853	Maidstone	Richard Records	0622 757 869
Croydon	Wax City	081 666 0708	**ESSEX**		
Ealing	Vinyl Mania	081 566 5244	Chelmsford	Vinyl Rythm	0245 346 731
Edgware	Cathy	081 906 2183	Essex	Upfront Promotions	0850 871 160
Edmonton	Roller Express	081 807 7345	Harlow	Papa	0279 432 270
Forest gate	De Underground	081 519 9682	Romford	Boogie Times	0708 727 029
Hackney	Wired For Sound	081 985 7531	**REGIONAL**		
Haringey	Music Power	071 652 3091	Basingstoke	Sight Sound & Motion	0256 812 266
Harrow	Record Centre	081 868 8637	Brighton	Nik	0273 622 204
Ilford	Music Power	081 478 2080	Bury St. Edmonds	Groovy Toones	0284 724 980
Kingston	Troublesome	081 547 0113	Cambridge	Streetwise	0223 300 496
Tottenham	Just For The Beat	081 885 2775	Canterbury	Richard Records	0227 765 930
Oxford Street	Razor Records	071 287 1695	Coventry	Retrieve	0203 550 750
Seven Kings	Bassline	081 590 8400	Dover	Hummingbird	0304 202 320
Soho	Black Market	071 437 0478	Hastings	Ricky	0424 424 214
South Woodford	Paradise	081 530 5538	Reading	Record Basement	0734 573 922
Walthamstow	Record Village	081 520 7331	Sevenoaks	Compact Disc	0732 740 889
			Slough	Slough Records	0753 526 194
			Southend	Soulman	0702 335 444

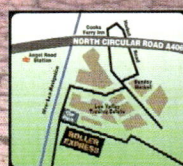

NORTH CIRCULAR ROAD A406

ROLLER EXPRESS

The Pirate Club would like to wish you all a Merry Christmas and a kicking New Year!

FREE COACH FROM TOTTENHAM HALE 9 to 12.00 midnight

ROAR ✦ NO UNDER 18'S ✦ ID's MAY BE REQUIRED ✦ STRINGENT SEARCHES ✦ NO ILLEGAL SUBSTANCES

NEW YEARS EVE TICKETS AVAILABLE ON THE NIGHT

PRINTED BY WESTWOOD PRESS 081-458095

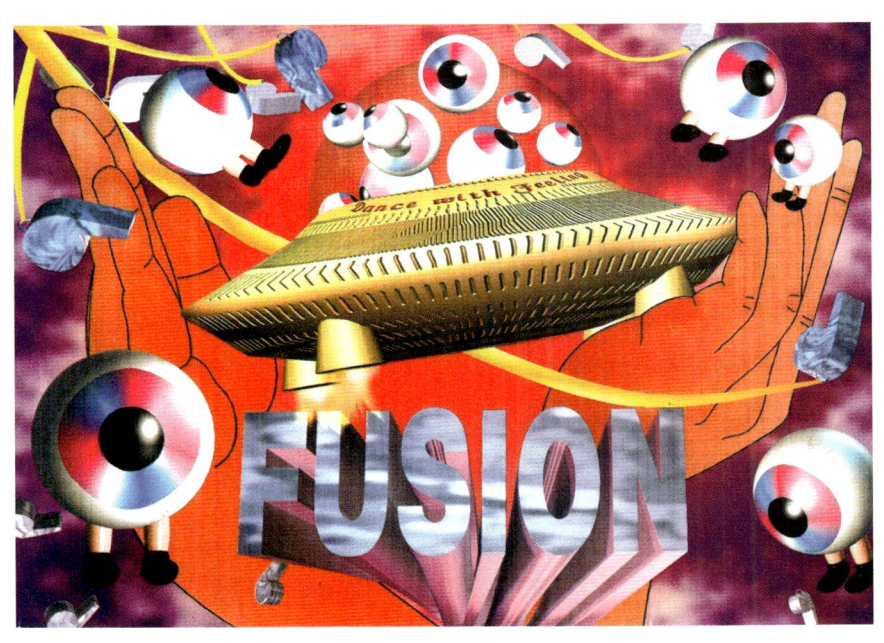

DANCE WITH FEELING
TAKES

FUSION
BACK TO IT'S UNDERGROUND HOME
THE MARQUEE
EVERY SATURDAY
STOP PRESS   STOP PRESS   STOP PRESS
ON SATURDAY 19th JUNE
WE WILL HAVE AN EXTENDED LICENSE - FUSION WILL RUN FROM
11pm - 6am ON THIS NIGHT DOOR PRICE £10/£8 MEM/£5 AFTER 3am

XX DJ'S IN YER FACE XX
on rotation
LONDON'S LEADING LADIES
DJ RAP   *   KILLER PUSSIES**

THE UK's MEANEST MEN

DJ HYPE	***	SLIPMAT
RAY KEITH	***	JOE 90
DEVIOUS D	***	DMS
TRIBAL 2	***	TORCHMAN
LEO	***	TRANSIT

11pm THE 6am LICENSE IS VERY CLOSE, SO HANG ON IN THERE! WE WILL HAVE OCCASIONAL TEMPORARY 6am NIGHTS BETWEEN NOW AND GETTING THE PERMANENT 6am LICENSE **3am**

FUSION ALL NIGHT OPTION
FUSION ALLNIGHTER VOUCHER ENTITLING YOU TO RAVE
ON ARRIVAL AT FUSION YOU WILL BE GIVEN A SPECIAL
FOR A FURTHER SEVEN HOURS AT SELECTED VENUES
FOR A MASSIVELY DISCOUNTED PRICE!
(AND WE MEAN MASSIVELY DISCOUNTED)

£6   FUSION   **£4** MEM's
at THE MARQUEE
CHARING CROSS RD, LONDON WC2
DANCE WITH FEELING INFO: 071 837 7151/0831 541037
LIPSMACKINGLY, FOOT STAMPINGLY, WHISTLE RAVEINGLY
W I C K E D !

D.T.P. PRESENTS

— fibreOPTIC —

THE SUMMER BALL

ON FRIDAY 19th JUNE 1992
10.00pm - 8.00am
AT THE ECLIPSE, LOWER FORD STREET, COVENTRY

NO ORDINARY PARTY, FIBREOPTIC PROMOTIONS WILL BE COMPLETELY TRANSFORMING THIS VENUE IN AN ATTEMPT TO BRING YOU SOMETHING A LITTLE BIT SPECIAL, SO JOIN WITH US, EXPERIENCE THE DIFFERENCE, FIBREOPTIC'S SUMMER BALL.

DJ's

STU ALLAN ● RATTY ● MICKEY FINN
ELLIS DEE ● DJ SS ● GROOVERIDER
LUKE ● SWAN'E ● FALLOUT ● PILGRIM
MCs ROBBIE DEE (FANTAZIA) ● SHOCK C

LIVE PAs ● NEBULA II ● ESSENCE ●

- LOWER FLOOR DJs -
TANGO ● NEIL TRIX ● TRANCE DANCE ● BLOD ● POWELY ● BEAR ● SHOT ONE ● COZ

ATTRACTIONS

20K TURBO SOUND ● MULTI COLOUR LASER SHOW ● UV & FIRE JUGGLERS
BALLOON DROP ● STATE OF THE ART LIGHTING & VISUAL IMAGERY
STILTWALKERS ● MULTI - LEVEL DANCE PLATFORMS ● CHAOTIC UV DECOR
FANCY DRESS DANCERS ● FLOURO BODY PAINTING ● UNICYCLIST

ENQUIRIES 0926 885551 ● 0203 555065 (24hr) ● VIP FAX 0203 632737

Tickets £15.00 PLUS BOOKING FEE
FROM OUTLETS & AGENTS LISTED BELOW

CREDIT CARD BOOKINGS
0733 60075

FOR MEMBERSHIP & MAILING LIST
SEND DETAILS TO:-
FIBREOPTIC PROMOTIONS
10 GLOUCESTER STREET
LEAMINGTON SPA, WARWICKSHIRE

BANBURY	CHALKY REC'S	0295 271190	MANCHESTER	EASTERN BLOCK RECORDS	061 228 6432
BIRMINGHAM	DEPOT	021 643 6045	MILTON KEYNES	WORLD BEATS	0908 310964
CHELTENHAM	CULT CLOTHING	0242 578376	NOTTINGHAM	JUST GROOVE RECORDS	0602 475008
COVENTRY	REVIVE	0203 550750	NORTHAMPTON	SPIN A DISC	0604 31144
COVENTRY	BANG IN TUNES	0203 559930	SHEFFIELD	WARP RECORDS	0742 757585
DAVENTRY	BATES	0327 77731	SHREWSBURY	RAINBOW RECS	0743 357058
DERBY	B.P.M.	0332 382038	STAMFORD	M & B RECORDS	0780 55289
EVESHAM	ALAN	0386 47844	STOKE	ENTROPY	0782 201499
KENILWORTH	TIM	0926 56735	STRATFORD	LOUISE	0789 415996
LEAMINGTON	FIBRE OPTIC RECS	0926 885551	W'HAMPTON	RUBY RED RECORDS	0902 771186
LEICESTER	5 HQ	0533 627475	WIGAN	MUSIC ZONE	0942 820 247
LEICESTER	B.P.M.	0533 624449			
LIVERPOOL	3 BEAT RECORDS	051 709 5533		MOONSHINE RECORDS - 0203 520739	
LUTON	SOUL SENSE	0582 23337		(OPEN ALL NIGHT. PAY ON THE NIGHT - OPPOSITE ECLIPSE)	

RESPECT AND THANKS TO: MICKEY (AMNESIA HOUSE) ● GIDEON, JAMES & NICK (FANTAZIA) ● CHRIS (MYTHOLOGY)
NEVILLE & LUKE (BANG IN TUNES) ● BRAD, BUD & SMITHY

Designed & Printed by C.P. Print (0203) 520050

NEW BEGINNINGS

DIGITAL FISH

KARMA SUTRA PRODUCTIONS

PRESENT

ENERGY

ON FRIDAY
29th NOVEMBER • 10PM-8AM
AT THE ECLIPSE CLUB, LOWER FORD STREET COVENTRY

ALL NIGHT!

MUSIC

ALL NIGHT!

Live P.A

CARL COX • JUMPING JACK FROST • MICKEY FINN
GROOVE RIDER • PHANTASY • LOGIC
BABY MO • DJ TORCH
MICKEY PARKES • MICKEY WILSON

ENERGY ARE CELEBRATING ONE YEAR AT THE ECLIPSE CLUB. WE WANT YOU, OUR FAITHFUL RAVERS, TO SPEND OUT BIRTHDAY PARTY WITH US. ENERGY AND ECLIPSE PUMPIN' ALL NIGHT WITH A TOP DJ LINE-UP, AND TO ADD TO THE ATMOSPHERE THERE WILL BE TOP GUEST APPEARANCES DURING THE NIGHT TO MAKE THIS THE BEST PARTY EVER SEEN AT THE ECLIPSE.

YOU KNOW WHAT TO EXPECT FROM OUR PROMOTIONS SO WE ARE NOT GOING TO HYPE IT UP, JUST SIMPLY BE THERE TO EXPERIENCE THE ANNUAL PARTY.

TICKET AGENTS

TIM - BASILDON 0268 527499 • DEPOT - BIRMINGHAM 021 643 6045 • PRIMADONNA - CAMBRIDGE 0223 353325 • MOONSHINE - COVENTRY 0203 520739 • POSTER PLACE - COVENTRY 0203 226176 • SUBLEVEL - GRIMSBY 0472 356601 • SNEAKERS - LEICESTER 0533 627475 • SOUL SENSE - LUTON 0582 23337 • SPIN-A-DISC - NORTHAMPTON 0604 31144 • ARCADE - NOTTINGHAM 0602 474932 • GROOVE RECORDS - NOTTINGHAM 0602 475008 • RICHARD - NORFOLK/SUFFOLK 0502 500536/0860 883194 • WORLD CLASS RECORDS - COLCHESTER 0206 768979 • ZENA - OXFORD 0865 66911 • STEVE JASON (CREDIT CARD HOTLINE) PETERBOROUGH 0733 60075 • HOMEBOYZ - SWINDON 0793 420467 • WORLD BEATS - MILTON KEYNES 0908 310964 • MICHAEL - CAMBRIDGE 0954 781928 • ERROL - TELFORD 0952 200761 • STEVE - WEST LONDON 0836 349493 • JAMIE/GEOFF - WEST MIDLANDS 0664 61480NEIL/ ANDY 0670 738565 NORTH EAST • TIME/STEVE NORTH WALES 0407 762347/760683 • JOHN - SOUTH WALES - 0792 290504 • RICHARD - SOUTH COAST 0903 208031 0860 444416 • JAMES - HUMBERSIDE 0482 25604 • TOM - HEREFORD & WORCESTER 0584 890010 • TONY - YORKSHIRE 0302 739414 • MATT - YORKSHIRE 0742 697134 • DARREN - ESSEX 0376 551049 or 0850 327029 • DEBBIE - REDDITCH 0527 501627 • JOHN – RPM PROMOTIONS 0831 226340

INFORMATION LINE – 0839 812323 MEMBERSHIP LINE 0839 812322
Urgent Enquiries & Letters send to: Suite 283, No 2 Old Brompton Road, London SW7 3DQ
Telephone Enquiries: 071-937 7854
Calls charged 34p per minute off peak and 45p peak

E<LIPS3 93 ·meets· DREAMSCAPE

on Saturday 19th June 1993

THE MEETING OF TWO MINDS

TWO OF THE MOST ESTABLISHED DANCE MUSIC ORGANISATIONS MEET IN THE EAST OF THE COUNTRY FOR THIS 1 OFF EVENT.

TO

be staged at East Anglia's

No1 Premier Venue

Cambridge Corn Exchange

9pm-6am

EST. eSP 1986

PROMOTIONS

GROOVE
PROMOTIONS

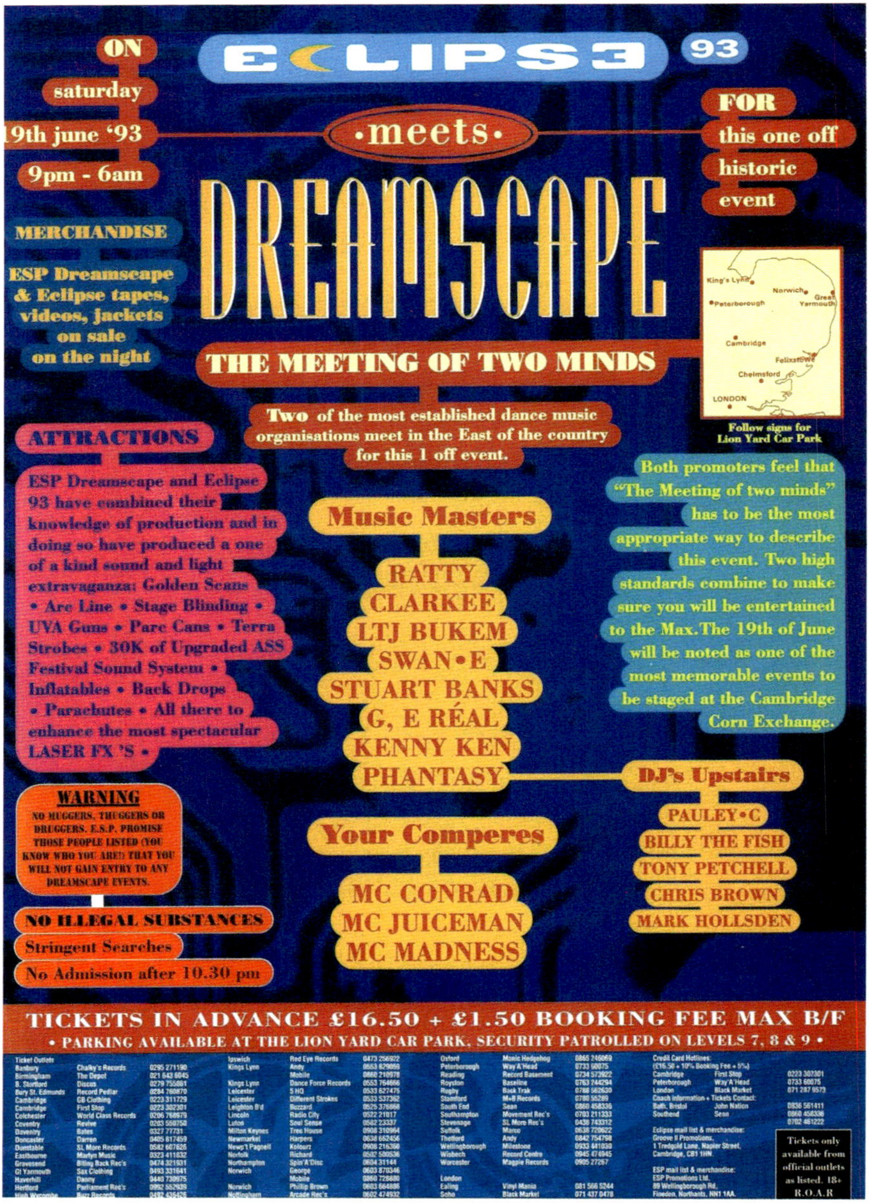

ECLIPS3 93

ON
saturday
19th june '93
9pm - 6am

FOR
this one off
historic
event

MERCHANDISE

ESP Dreamscape & Eclipse tapes, videos, jackets on sale on the night

DREAMSCAPE

THE MEETING OF TWO MINDS

Follow signs for Lion Yard Car Park

Two of the most established dance music organisations meet in the East of the country for this 1 off event.

ATTRACTIONS

ESP Dreamscape and Eclipse 93 have combined their knowledge of production and in doing so have produced a one of a kind sound and light extravaganza: Golden Scans • Arc Line • Stage Blinding • UVA Guns • Parc Cans • Terra Strobes • 30K of Upgraded ASS Festival Sound System • Inflatables • Back Drops • Parachutes • All there to enhance the most spectacular LASER FX 'S •

Both promoters feel that "The Meeting of two minds" has to be the most appropriate way to describe this event. Two high standards combine to make sure you will be entertained to the Max. The 19th of June will be noted as one of the most memorable events to be staged at the Cambridge Corn Exchange.

Music Masters

RATTY
CLARKEE
LTJ BUKEM
SWAN • E
STUART BANKS
G, E RÉAL
KENNY KEN
PHANTASY

DJ's Upstairs

PAULEY • C
BILLY THE FISH
TONY PETCHELL
CHRIS BROWN
MARK HOLLSDEN

WARNING
NO HUGGERS, THUGGERS OR DRUGGERS. E.S.P. PROMISE THOSE PEOPLE LISTED (YOU KNOW WHO YOU ARE) THAT YOU WILL NOT GAIN ENTRY TO ANY DREAMSCAPE EVENTS.

NO ILLEGAL SUBSTANCES

Stringent Searches

No Admission after 10.30 pm

Your Comperes

MC CONRAD
MC JUICEMAN
MC MADNESS

TICKETS IN ADVANCE £16.50 + £1.50 BOOKING FEE MAX B/F
• PARKING AVAILABLE AT THE LION YARD CAR PARK, SECURITY PATROLLED ON LEVELS 7, 8 & 9 •

Tickets only available from official outlets as listed. 18+

R.O.A.R.

CRYSTAL CLEAR

PRESENTS

THE

WAREHOUSE

CONCEPT

CRYSTAL CLEAR PROMOTIONS

THE WARE HOUSE CONCEPT

Friday 27th January 1995 - 8pm till 2am

AT THE WAREHOUSE, UNION STREET, PLYMOUTH

For your pleasure... total crowd pleasers!

SY

(The one and only)
1-2

DOUGAL

(The ultimate happy man)
11-12

DESTRUCTION

(Plymouth's No.1, Happy as Larry)
12-1

PULSE   FUSION   KEV ROSE   DJ HARRY

The Crystal Clear policy:-
We have a music policy which only delivers the goods to the people. No undanceable shite!
Top tunes, delivered in top style by the nations finest, across the board, but most definetly on the happy tip.

MC's: *MARCO, QUEST & some very special guests!*

Are you Clear?

ATTRACTIONS

The full monty... 15k of sound, Laser, VR screens, Full backdrops and transformation, Smoke galore,
Arc projections, Friendly security, Merchandising ... all the frills and more.

THE REALLY GOOD NEWS

TICKET £5 +bk fee   DOOR £6 b4 9pm

No one offers you more, for less...
High production-low cost
Setting the standard in 95'
Over 18's only   ROAR Searches on entry
No attitudes, No stress, Just happy faces please!

ALL DJ'S ARE CONFIRMED & CONTRACTED AND CONTRACTS CAN BE SEEN AT ALL OUTLETS.

TICKET OUTLETS :

MUSIC BOX	0752 361920	URBAN COLLECTIVE	0752 256390
RIVAL RECORDS	0752 221952	SOUNDZ (TORQUAY)	0803 211097
I.D. (TORQUAY)	0803 214368	UPFRONT (BARNSTABLE)	0271 74187
REPLAY (BRISTOL)	0272 259840	MIGHTY FORCE (EXETER)	0392 433844
PHASE 2 (LISKEARD)	0579 347292	PUKKA MUSIC (NEWQUAY)	0637 879384

Regards 2 : The Crystal Clear family, Dynamix, SLIPMATT, CLARKEE, RAMOS, MASTERVIBE, APACHE,
SCORPIO, KENNY, SBC Crew, SONIA & the baby, LISA, AWESOME Records (JJ), RSR Records(Alex), ROLY(ESP),
Kev 4 the flyer and everyone who has supported us, including are loyal followers from day one...You shall be rewarded!

CRYPTONITE

presents

A QUANTUM LEAP

SATURDAY, APRIL 10th, 1993
9 p.m. – 7 a.m.
BANK HOLIDAY WEEKEND

The Sanctuary Music Arena
Milton Keynes

CRYPTONITE

SATURDAY, APRIL 10th, 1993 — 9 p.m. – 7 a.m.
AT THE SANCTUARY, V7 SAXON GATE, DENBIGH, MILTON KEYNES
BANK HOLIDAY WEEKEND

CRYPTONITE HERALDS THE ARRIVAL OF SPRING WITH A **'QUANTUM LEAP'** THAT WILL ENERGISE YOU INTO A NEW SEASON AND A NEW BEGINNING ON THE FIRST-EVER LICENSED ALL-NIGHT SATURDAY AT THE SANCTUARY MUSIC ARENA (THE LARGEST PURPOSE-BUILT DANCE VENUE IN ENGLAND) THIS 22,000 SQ. FT WAREHOUSE CONSISTS OF TWO ARENAS WITH A BALCONY OVERLOOKING THE MAIN DANCEFLOOR. THE VENUE ALSO FEATURES THE LARGEST FULLY INSTALLED SUSPENDED SOUND SYSTEM, CUSTOM-MADE DANCE PLATFORMS WITH BUILT-IN SUB-BASS, ALL 50K OF RENEGADE SOUND.

MAIN ARENA

GROOVERIDER - MICKEY FINN - RATTY - FABIO - RANDALL
LTJ BUKEM - KENNY KEN - DONOVAN 'BAD BOY' SMITH
TAYLA - M.C. MAGIKA

P.A.s

BUGG KHAN & THE PLASTIC JAM - NEW CLASS A
LAUNCHING THEIR NEW E.P. (LABELLO BLANCO RECORDINGS)
ORCA PERFORMING DANCES WITH DOLPHINS (LUCKY SPIN RECORDINGS)

ARENA 2 ("THE HOUSE THAT JACK BUILT")
MATT JAM LAMONT - RICHIE FINGERS - FACE
FRANKIE 'SHAG' BONES - MATT MAURICE
LIVE PERCUSSION "BONGO BEDLAM"
ALL D.J.s BOOKED THROUGH 'FLUID MOTION' – 071-733 7069
SPECIAL THANKS TO GROOVE CONNECTION

ATTRACTIONS

SHOCKING LIGHT SHOW INCORPORATING GOLDEN SCANS, TERRA STROBES, MOONBEAMS – AMAZING 3-D COMPUTER ANIMATED PROJECTIONS – TWIN-HEAD MULTI-COLOUR LASER SYSTEM – DANCE PLATFORMS – 3,000 CAPACITY – MERCHANDISING – DANCERS – TWO LICENSED BARS – STAGE SHOW TO IMPRESS – CHILLOUT – FRIENDLY SECURITY – SPECIAL SURPRISES IN STORE ON THE NIGHT AND AN EASTER BUNNY HUNT IN THE CAR PARK!

ADVANCE TICKETS: £15.00
+ BOOKING FEE

INFORMATION AND TRAVEL — 081-892 0199   081-744 9989
CREDIT CARD HOTLINE   FIRST STOP BOX OFFICE 0223 302301

OUTLETS

ANDOVER	EARWAX	0264 337 236
BALDOCK	TUFFCUTS	0462 732 879
BANBURY	CHALKIES RECORDS	0295 271 190
BASILDON	CAROUSEL (MISSION)	0268 289 016
BASINGSTOKE	FUNKY BUBBLE	0256 81366
BEDFORD	ANDY'S RECORDS	0234 342 784
BENFLEET	ARMAGEDDON	0268 795 668
BIRMINGHAM	THE DEPOT	021-643 6045
BISHOPS STORTFORD	DISCUS	0279 755 861
BOURNEMOUTH	MET 2	0202 315 535
BRIGHTON	ROUNDER RECORDS	0273 325 440
BRISTOL	TRIBE OF THREE	0272 225 200
BROMLEY	BLUEBIRD RECORDS	081-313 3413
CAMBRIDGE	FIRST STOP	0223 302 301
CARDIFF	I CLAUDIUS	0222 222 215
CHELMSFORD	THE CLAN	0245 256 796
CHELTENHAM	CULT CLOTHING	0242 250 044
COLCHESTER	WORLD CLASS	0206 768 979
COVENTRY	BANGIN TUNES	0203 559 930
DAVENTRY	BATES CLOTHING	0327 77731
DERBY	BPM RECORDS	0332 382 038
DUNSTABLE	CASUAL SOUNDS	0582 600 267
EPSOM	FIRST CUTS	0372 478 881
GLOUCESTER	OHM	0452 382 561
GUILDFORD	DANCE 2	0483 451 002
HEMEL HEMPSTEAD	RECORD SHACK	0442 255 186

HIGH WYCOMBE	BUZZ RECORDS	0494 436 426
HITCHIN	PARLIAMENT RECORDS	0462 459 058
IPSWICH	RED EYE	0473 256 922
KINGS LYNN	ANDY'S RECORDS	0553 760 790
LEAMINGTON SPA	FIBRE OPTIC	0926 885 551
LEICESTER	5 HQ	0533 627 475
LIVERPOOL	3 BEAT	051-707 1669
LUTON	SOUL SENSE	0582 23337
MANCHESTER	SPIN INN	061-834 5383
MILTON KEYNES	TREE HOUSE	0908 310 964
MILTON KEYNES	THE SANCTUARY	0908 368 984
MILTON KEYNES	KOLOURZ	0908 216 360
NORTHAMPTON	SPIN-A-DISC	0604 31144
NORWICH	SOUND CLASH	0603 761 004
NOTTINGHAM	ARCADE RECORDS	0602 674 932
OXFORD	MANIC HEDGEHOG	0865 246 069
PETERBOROUGH	WAY AHEAD	0733 60075
READING	RECORD BASEMENT	0734 573 922
SLOUGH	SLOUGH RECORDS	0753 528 194
SOUTHEND	ALTERED STATES	0702 603 733
SOUTHAMPTON	MOVEMENT RECORDS	0703 211 333
STAFFORD	LOTUS RECORDS	0785 43910
SWINDON	RIVAL RECORDS	0793 542 093
WESTON-S-MARE	BARBER RECORDS	0934 644 464
WISBECH	RECORD STORM	0945 474 945
WOLVERHAMPTON	RUBY RED	0902 29674

LONDON OUTLETS

CAMDEN	ZOOM	071-267 4479
CENTRAL	MASH/PASSION	071-287 1695
CHELSEA	LUCKY SPIN	071-351 6853
CROYDON	WAX CITY	081-655 0708
EALING	VINYL	081-866 5244
FOREST GATE	DE UNDERGROUND	081-519 9982
ILFORD	MUSIC	081-478 2080
KINGSTON	TROUBLESOME RECORDS	081-547 0113

LONDON AGENTS

NORTH LONDON	WARREN	081-459 0071
STREATHAM	MARK	081-677 1591

UK AGENTS

LUTON	JULIE	0582 391 690
NORFOLK	RICHARD	0502 500 536
WATFORD	BECKY	0923 229 276

ORACLE NATIONWIDE AGENTS & FLYING NETWORK

BIRMINGHAM	RALF	021-384 1916
BOURNEMOUTH	CAMIE	0202 547 250
BRISTOL	JOHN	0836 561 411
CAMBRIDGE	CLAIRE	0440 706 602
CORBY	PAUL	0536 60868
DERBY	KEV	0831 554 528
HIGH WYCOMBE	SEAN	0494 444 769
LINCOLN	LISA	0522 500 372
MILTON KEYNES	SEAN	0908 662 170
OXFORD	ANDY	0865 744 334
WALSALL	TIM	0922 613 503

R.O.A.R. – NO ILLEGAL SUBSTANCES – STRINGENT SEARCHES UPON ENTRY – SORRY, NO UNDER-EIGHTEENS
PRODUCTION BROUGHT TO YOU BY CRYPTONITE IN ASSOCIATION WITH TALISMAN

EST 1989

AMNESIA HOUSE

U.K. PROMOTIONS ON

FRIDAY 8TH MAY 1992

AT THE

FROM 9PM — TILL 8AM

ECLIPSE

LOWER FORD STREET, COVENTRY

THE AMNESIA CREW NOW PROUDLY PRESENTS OUR SECOND ALL NIGHTER AT THE ECLIPSE WITH A TOTALLY DIFFERENT SET UP AND DJ LINE-UP, AS WE CONTINUE TO BUILD UP TOWARDS OUR MASSIVE OPEN AIR SUMMER EVENT.

LIGHT & SOUND SORTED AS USUAL

BAD BOYS ON THE NIGHT

2 FLOORS 2 SOUND SYSTEMS 2 GOOD TO MISS

MAIN ARENA

PARKES & WILSON
ECLIPSE

JUMPING JACK FROST
INTER DANCE

GROOVE RIDER
AMNESIA

RAY KEITH
LONDON

CARL COX
3 DEX

STU ALLAN
MANCHESTER

SWAN-E
PERCEPTION

RON
LONDON

NAMES TO LOOK OUT FOR — **LOWER FLOOR** — NAMES TO LOOK OUT FOR

DEAN
HOME BOY

TAYLOR
LONDON

REGGIE P
HOME BOY

SHOCK C
ECLIPSE

MARK 1
ALTERN 8

CARL WILLIAMS
ECLIPSE

DOCTOR H
DAVENTRY

MCs **LOUD 'N' NASTY & MAN PARRIS**
AMNESIA

PLUS MC **ROBBIE DEE**
FANTASIA

TICKET PRICE £15
PLUS BOOKING FEE

L.T.D. AMOUNT OF TICKETS
MORE ON THE DOOR IF AVAILIABLE
INQUIRIES:- 0926 885551 OR 0203 559930

BEWARE OF FORGERIES

CREDIT CARD BOOKING'S 0733 60075 ★ **OUTLETS & AGENTS**

BANBURY	CHALKY REC'S	0295 271190	MILTON KEYNES	WORLD BEATS	0908 310964
BIRMINGHAM	DEPOT	021 643 6045	NOTTINGHAM	JUST GROOVE RECORDS	0602 475008
COVENTRY	BANG IN TUNES	0203 559930	NORTHAMPTON	SPIN A DISC	0604 31144
DAVENTRY	BATES	0327 77731	SHEFFIELD	WARP RECORDS	0742 757585
DERBY	B.P.M.	0332 382038	SHREWSBURY	RAINBOW REC'S	0743 357058
KETTERING	KLASSI REC'S	0536 412107	STAMFORD	M & B RECORDS	0780 55289
LEAMINGTON	FIBRE OPTIC REC'S	0926 885551	STOKE	ENTROPY	0782 201499
LEICESTER	B.P.M.	0533 624449	WALSALL	ZOOT CLOTHING	0922 720178
LIVERPOOL	3 BEAT RECORDS	051 709 5533	W'HAMPTON	RUBY RED RECORDS	0902 771186
LUTON	SOUL SENSE	0582 23337	WIGAN	MUSIC ZONE	0942 820 247
MANCHESTER	EASTERN BLOCK RECORDS	061 228 6432			

LOOK OUT FOR OUR MASSIVE SUMMER TIME RAVE COMING SOON

PRINTED BY C. P. PRINT SERVICES, COVENTRY, TEL:- (0203) 520050

Seduction

Opening 11th Dec 92
Every Friday 10pm until 6am

In the beginning there was house, the backbone of music. Pyramid Promotions is proud to announce the revival of the originator, 8 hours of true pure house supported by one of its newer sisters, Garage, each and every Friday. The Lazerdrome is London's most unique venue, a labyrinth of confusion and illusion.

THE SEDUCERS:

HOUSE ARENA	GARAGE SUITE
11TH DECEMBER	
Dominic	Master P, Lindon C
Face	Matt 'Jam' Lamont
Richie Fingers	Bobby & Steve, Chrissy T
18TH DECEMBER	
Frankie 'Shag' Bones	Aubury, Tony Trax
Judge Jules	Matt 'Jam' Lamont
Alex P	Master P
8TH JANUARY	
Tintin	Stuart C McClellan
Face	Louis G & G Max
Matthew B	Bobby & Steve
15TH JANUARY	
Tamsin	Master P, Mr Benn
Dominic	Stuart Dashwood
Shaggy & Breeze	Chrissy T

LIVE P.A.S TO BE CONFIRMED

LAZERDROME
267 RYE LANE
LONDON SE15

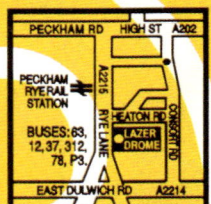

$5 ON THE DOOR
$3 AFTER 3.30AM
INFO (071) 732 5047

R.O.A.R.
No illegal substances.
No alcohol.

11th SEPT

DREAM PROMOTIONS (UK)
Proudly Presents

DREAM ZONE TOO

AT THE
LEAS CLIFF HALL, FOLKSTONE, KENT, Nr. PAVILION.

VENUE

DREAM PROMOTIONS HAVE SPENT 6 MONTHS FINDING A VENUE TO SUIT YOU FOR THE TYPE OF EVENTS WE THINK YOU WILL ENJOY THIS IS A ONE OFF CONCERT AT THIS VENUE, NEVER AGAIN WILL YOU GET SO MUCH FOR SO LITTLE?

LIVE ON STAGE

P.A.s

THESE P.A.s HAVE BEEN PICKED FOR THEIR CONSTANT APPEAR-ANCES IN THE TOP 10 UNDER-GROUND DANCE CHARTS IN AND AROUND LONDONS TOP RECORD SHOPS. THEY ARE THE BEST AROUND.

RUFIGE KRU   4 HERO
Teminator   performing their
/St. Angel   new E.P.
SLAMMIN VINYL
Back on Wax

VINYL POSTERS

D.J.s

THESE D.J.s CHOSEN FOR THEIR SUCCESS AROUND ENGLAND. THEY ARE THE PEOPLES CHOICE. RESPECT!

L.T.J. BUKEM   ELLIS-DEE
Fantazia/Universe   Raindance
BUZZKIRK   /World Dance
Dream Zone/Ki Ki'S

ATTRACTIONS

LAZERS

WE AT DREAM PROMOTIONS AGREE THAT TO GET A GOOD ATMOSPHERE RAVERS DON'T WANT A VERY BRIGHT VENUE "THE DARKER THE BETTER" SO THIS WILL BE A STRICTLY LAZERS AND STROBES FOR A NIGHT. WE HOPE YOU APPROVE?

1 FULL 7 COLOUR 8 WATT
1 RED - 3 GREEN AND BLUE
STROBES
SMOKE - BACKDROPS
REFRESHMENTS- CLOAK ROOMS
TOILET FACILITIES

BREATING THE BASS

WICKED SYSTEMS WILL BE HOSTING OUR PA SYSTEM. THIS IS THE PAYBACK FOR ATOMICS WE PROMISE BASS IN YA FACE (NO FALSE PROMISES).

DEAR RAVER

WE AT DREAM PROMOTIONS WOULD JUST LIKE TO SAY WE DO "NOT" AGREE WITH FLYERS FULL OF BULLSHIT-ATTRACTIONS THAT AREN'T THERE, SO WE ARE GIVING THE REAL DEAL AT THE RIGHT PRICE. PLEASE ARRIVE EARLY DOORS OPEN AT 8.00 P.M. NO ILLE-GAL SUBSTANCES, NO ALCOHOL, I.D. MAY BE REQUIRED.

ENQUIRIES RING:
WARREN 0374 108562. ADDY 0850 400104. KEITH 0233 628054

TO THE REAL PROMOTERS: WORLD DANCE - AWOL - ELEVATION - UTOPIA AND LIFE
REINFORCED - GROOVE CONNECTIONS "RESPECT"

AGENTS (KENT)

STEVE	(0303) 270333	FOLKSTONE
WARREN	(0374) 108562	KENT
KEITH	(0233) 628054	ASHFORD
ADDY	(0850) 400104	ASHFORD
JAMES	(0795) 521634	SITTINGBOURNE
ALISON	(0634) 294581	STROOD

REGIONAL & LONDON

JULIE	(0252) 714636	SLOUGH
NINA	(081) 309 1998	DARTFORD
STACY	(081) 309 2729	ORPINGTON

OUTLETS

DREAM PROMOTIONS HQ	(0374) 108562	KENT
RICHARDS RECORDS	(0233) 629106	ASHFORD
RICHARDS RECORDS	(0622) 661787	MAIDSTONE
RICHARDS RECORDS	(0622) 681787	MAIDSTONE
HUMMINGBIRD RECORDS	(0227) 452826	CANTERBURY
HUMMINGBIRD RECORDS	(0227) 243836	CANTERBURY
FAT ALBERTS	(0277) 784055	FOLKSTONE
PLASTIC SURGERY TOO	(0622) 661757	CANTERBURY
METRO MUSIC	(0622) 423727	GRAVESEND
WHITE LABEL RECORDS	(0795) 142891	MAIDSTONE
LEES CLIFF BOX OFFICE	(0303) 253193	FOLKSTONE

AGENTS AND OUTLETS

OUTLETS LONDON & REGIONAL

BERRY	(081) 304 0171	BROMLEY
BLUE HEATH	(081) 313 3413	BLUE
BLACK MARKET	(071) 437 0478	CENTRAL LONDON
VINYL-PASSION	(071) 287 1942	CENTRAL LONDON
UNITY-PASSION	(071) 734 2746	CENTRAL LONDON
MUSIC POWER	(081) 478 2060	ILFORD
MUSIC CENTRE	(081) 868 8637	HARROW
MUSIC POWER	(081) 800 6113	HARRINGAY

TICKETS
£8.50
INC. BOOKING
FEE 10% MAX

MORE ON
THE DOOR

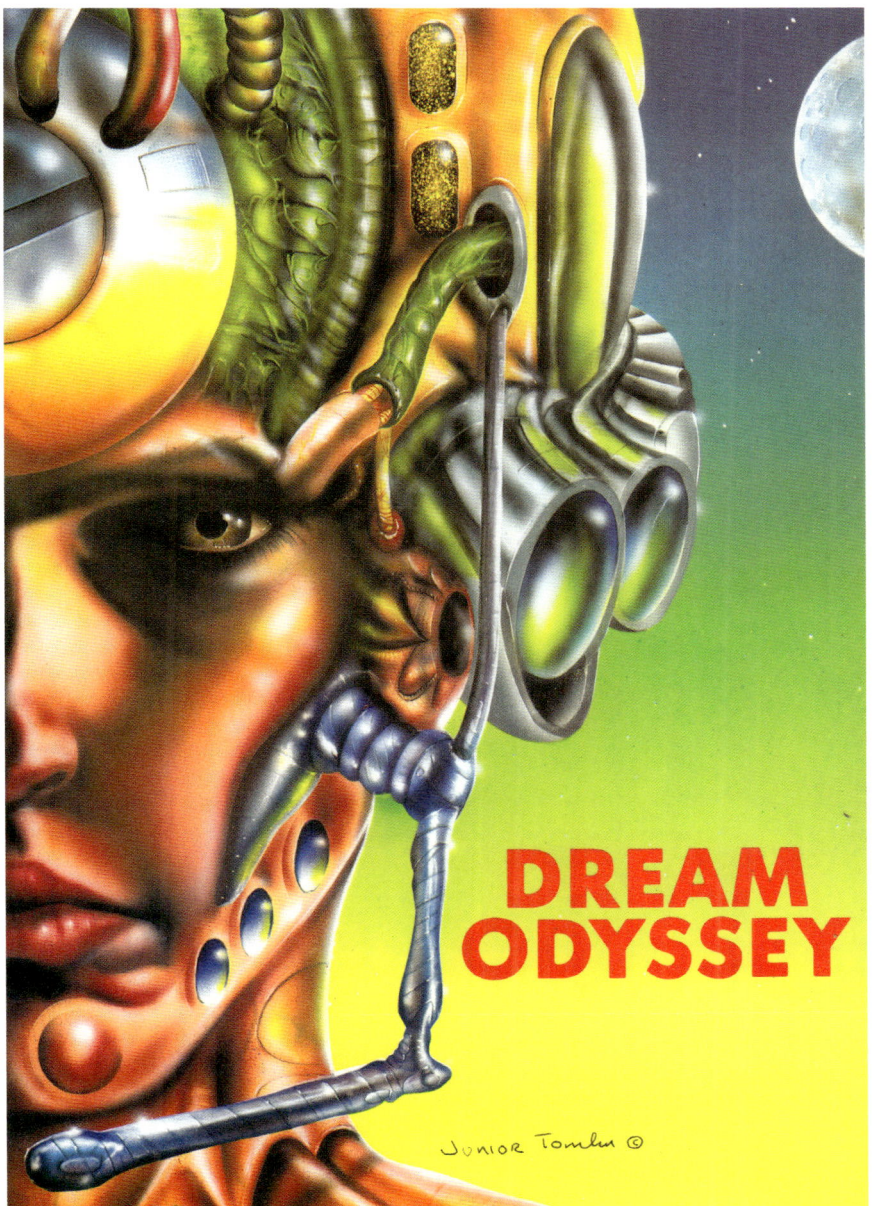

DREAM
ODYSSEY

Junior Tomlin ©

MAIN ROOM

"Upfront Break Beat/Junglist and Hardcore Classics"

PA's

Ratpack, Divine Inspiration, Tribal 2, The Dance, Twin Bass, The Charm, Friends United, O.D.C. Professional Dancers.

DJ's

Joe '90, Tasmin – Queen of Hardcore, DJ Excel, Lt. Stitch, E-Z Man, Jimmy J, DJ Trax, The Jinx, DJ Dove, DJ Lomax, Jack Horner, Vinyl Sex, DJ Ian Andrew, DJ Jester, Big Dave.

MC's

Chalkie White, MC Excel, MC Trance.

BASEMENT

"Steaming Hardcore"

DJ's

Ian Andrew, Tasmin – Queen of Hardcore, The Jinx.

ATTIC

"Classic Club Anthems/Summer of 89 Tunes"

DJ's

The Operator, DJ Gordon Gee, E-Z Man.

FOR YOU WHO WERE THERE FROM THE BEGINNING. . . . .WHO MADE THE DREAM POSSIBLE, AND YOU WHO HAVE RECENTLY JOINED AND HELPED RECAPTURE THE SPIRIT OF THE RAVESCENE BACK FROM THE OMINOUS DEPTHS OF DESTRUCTION. . . . .

We are asking for *YOUR* support in gathering together your friends to join our underground movement, to make this the event of a lifetime.

Attend this rave extravaganza, and unite the movement which leads the way to setting new standards. For here: NO "ATTITUDE" WILL BE TOLERATED. We are guaranteeing you 12 solid hours of happy, friendly, unequalled pleasure, amongst genuine ravers, who like yourself, totally know the koo.

We at Divine Inspiration Promotions, have gone to great lengths to ensure your safety and happiness are our top priorities.

Everything right down to all PA's and DJ's have been thoroughly vetted to remove the "It'll be all right on the night" dilema that most raves operate on, which teamed with a 35K Turbobass sound system, the cheapest possible admission price (£5) and a DJ line-up second to none ensures you, a top event. Therefore you will only have yourself to blame if you don't have a wicked time. Unlike other greedy promoters, we are not in this for a fast buck, we want to earn your loyalty and respect.

So attend this event on Sunday the 7th March 1993 at THE LABRINTH, 12 Dalston Lane E8, 12 noon – 12 pm and MAKE YOUR DREAM. . . . . BECOME A REALITY . . . . 'COS ONLY YOU HAVE THE POWER TO CHANGE THE FUTURE.

NOTE: *To all who have supported, encouraged and inspired me (and you know who you are!) Respect and love to you. You are the 'Hardcore' by contributing your time you care enough to set new standards for the future. You will never be forgotten*

♡ *fathom*
x

Illustrations by Junior Tomlinson Tel: 081 968 5784

DREAM PROMOTIONS (UK) PROUDLY PRESENTS
THE LAST EVER

DREAM ZONE

AT THE

ATOMICS DANCE VENUE,HART STREET,MAIDSTONE KENT

SATURDAY 27th FEBURARY

FEATURING

CARL COX
D.J BUZZKIRK
KILLER PUSSIES

KISS FM

D.J BONES
KIKIS/DREAM ZONE

D.J EXCEL
LOVE OF LIFE/ILLUSION

ATTRACTIONS

Lazers,
*
Flower Strobes
*
Smoke
*
Terror Strobes
*
Arc Lines
*
Different Level Floors
*
3 Fully Licensed Bars
*
Lazer Backdrops
*
All D.J.'s 100% Confirmed
*
Firm But Friendly Security
*
Hot Food

HOW TO GET THERE

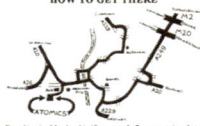

Free Atomics Membership if you supply 2 passport size photos

A real big thanks to the 1,000's of ravers who
have supported **DREAM ZONE.** As well
you know, our lights, lazers and DJ's are
always 100% confirmed, no ripoffs here.
Although this is the last **DREAM ZONE** at
ATOMICS we're at a new venue very soon.
**FIND OUT ON THE NIGHT WHERE!
R.O.A.R. STRICTLY NO ILLEGAL
SUBSTANCES PARTY PEOPLE ONLY.**

**TICKETS £6.50
NO GUEST LIST
FOR COMPLIMENTARY
TICKETS RING:
RICHARD(0531) 357723**

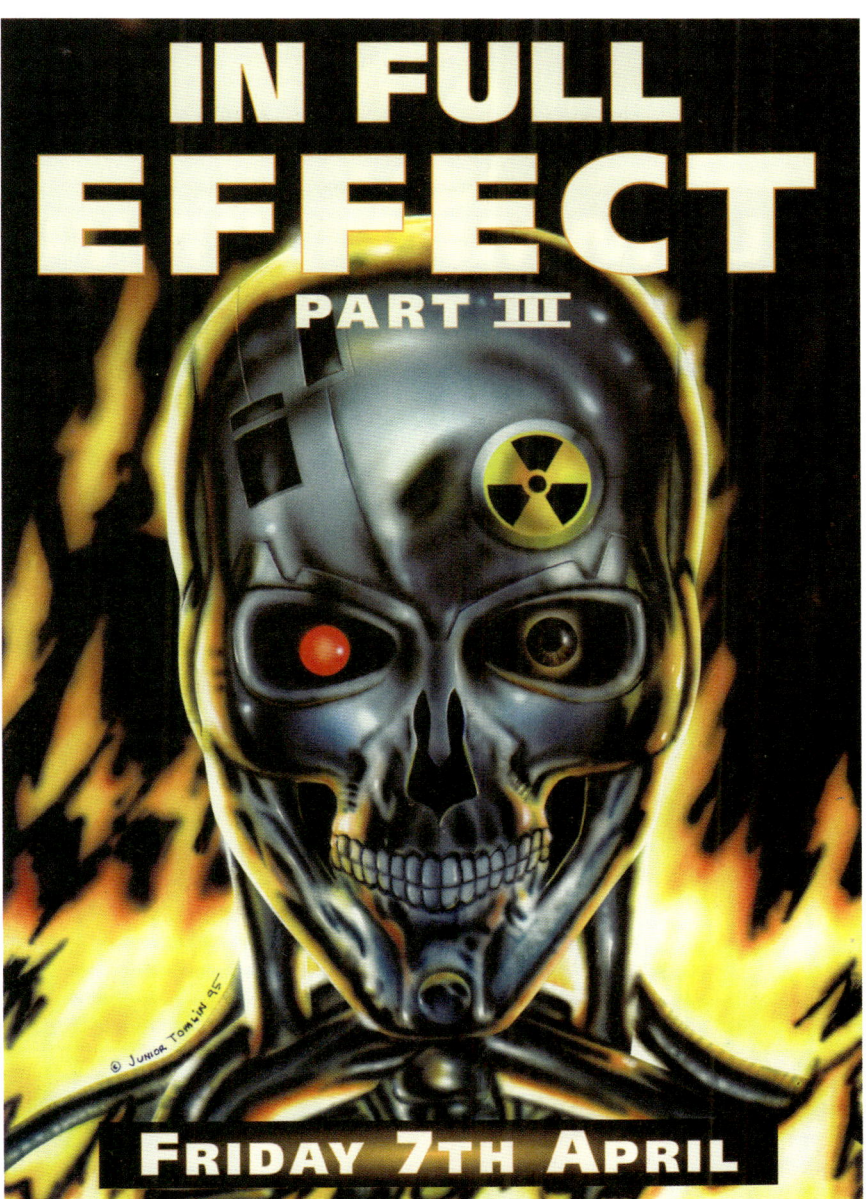

£10 ON THE DOOR

£10 ON THE DOOR

SLAMMIN' VINYL

IN FULL EFFECT

PART III

FRIDAY 7th APRIL 9-6 AM ALL NIGHT

at **THE RHYTHM STATION**

STATION ROAD , ALDERSHOT, HAMPSHIRE

THOSE WHO ATTENDED OUR LAST EVENT ON THE 3RD MARCH KNOW THAT WE KNOW HOW TO PUT ON A PARTY !!! REMEMBER, WE ARE THE ONLY PROMOTERS AT THE RHYTHM STATION TO ALWAYS

DOUBLE THE SOUND, ALWAYS DOUBLE THE LIGHTING & ALWAYS BRING TO YOU THE MOST EXCLUSIVE & UPFRONT PA'S + DJ'S .WITH 12 DJS AND TWO MASSIVE PA'S FOR ONLY £10 YOU CAN'T AFFORD TO MISS IT !!!!!

SY - RAMOS - BRISK - UNKNOWN
CLARKEE - BILLY BUNTER
HIXXY - MR HYDE - JIMMY J
RED ALERT (BACK 2 BACK) MIKE SLAMMER
MC'S - ADRENALIN - SMILEY

FOR THE 1ST TIME EVER AT THE RHYTHM STATION - P.A BY SMD + THE SLAMMIN' VINYL P.A FEATURING BRAND NEW TRACKS BY VINYLGROOVER & DJ SLAM
100 % MORE SOUND MULTICOLOURED LAZERS + FX
LICENSED BAR + SECURE PARKING.

DJ BRISK APOLOGISES FOR HIS ABSENCE ON THE 3rd OF MARCH THIS TIME 100% CONFIRMED

HOUSE & GARAGE & CLASSICS UPSTAIRS COURTESY OF REMIX RECORDS LONDON'S Nº1

INFO. LINES:-
0850 - 700983
0374 - 480374

YET AGAIN WE HAVE A FULL RANGE OF MERCHANDISE & RECORDS FOR SALE AT BARGAIN PRICES

ILLUSTRATION , LAYOUT AND DESIGN **JUNIOR TOMLIN**

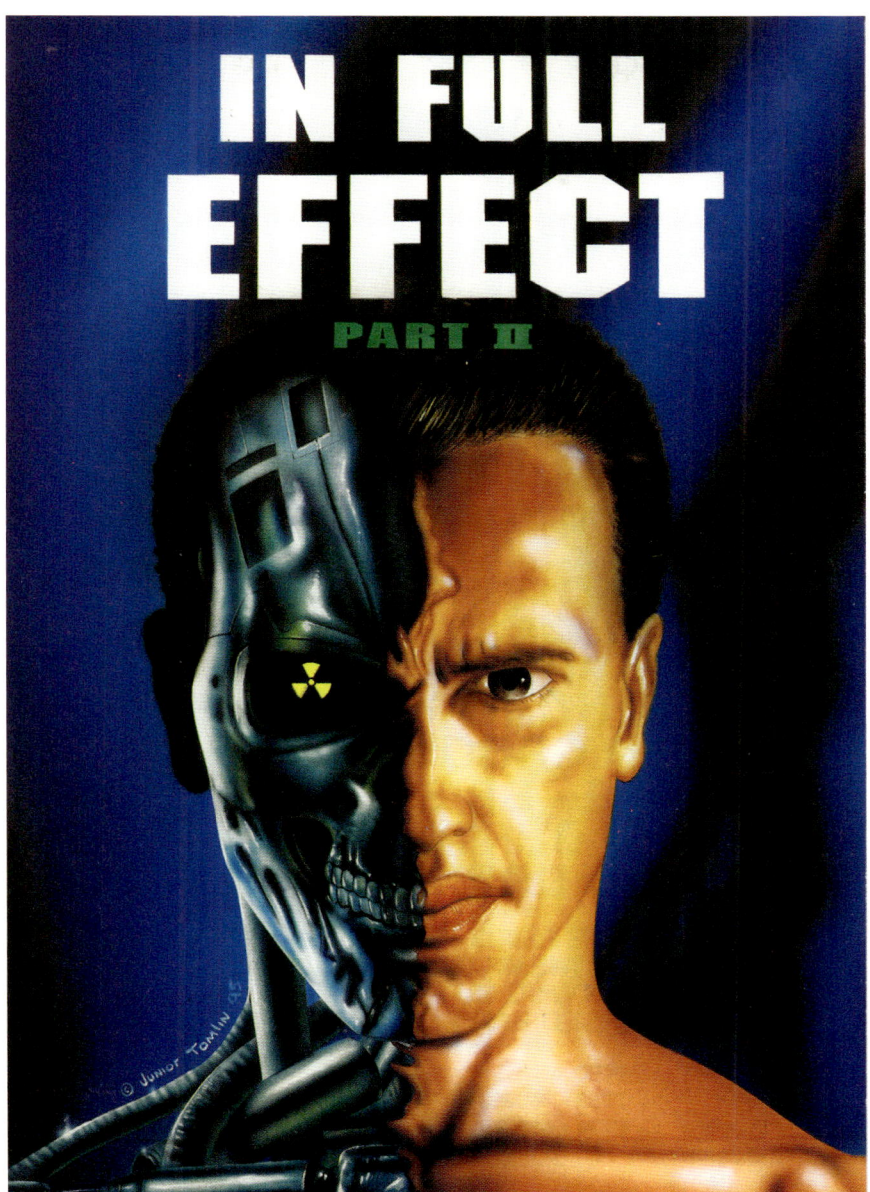

£10 ON THE DOOR

£10 ON THE DOOR

SLAMMIN' VINYL
presents
IN FULL EFFECT
PART II

FRIDAY 3RD MARCH 9-6 AM ALL NIGHT
at THE RHYTHM STATION
STATION ROAD , ALDERSHOT, HAMPSHIRE

HERE WE GO AGAIN WITH IN EFFECT PT II!!!! BRINGING YOU THE BEST IN HAPPY HARDCORE & BOUNCY TECHNO WITH 11 FULLY CONFIRMED DJ'S & A LIVE & EXCLUSIVE PA FROM REMIX RECORDS. ONCE MORE WE ARE SETTING THE HIGHEST PRODUCTION STANDARDS WITH A 100% EXPANDED SOUND SYSTEM & A DAZZLING ARRAY OF LIGHTS & MULTI - COLOURED LAZERS. WITH 11 DJ'S FOR ONLY A TENNER MAKE SURE YOU'RE THERE EARLY BECAUSE YOU KNOW ITS GONNA **BE RAMMED!!!!**

SY - DOUGAL - RAMOS- HYPE
VINYLGROOVER - DRUID
CLARKEE - BRISK - RED ALERT
BILLY BUNTER - JIMMY J
MC'S - ADRENALIN - SMILEY

REMIX RECORDS

LIVE + EXCLUSIVE REMIX RECORDS PA FEATURING THE HARDCORE ANTHEMS 'TAKE ME AWAY' +' SIX DAYS'. 100 % MORE SOUND MULTICOLOURED LAZERS +FX LICENSED BAR + SECURE PARKING.

HOUSE & GARAGE ALL NIGHT UPSTAIRS	**INFO. LINES:-** 0850 - 700983 0374 - 480374 	**YET AGAIN WE HAVE A FULL RANGE OF MERCHANDISE & RECORDS FOR SALE AT BARGAIN PRICES**

£10 on the door

£10 on the door

SLAMMIN' VINYL
presents

IN FULL EFFECT

ON FRI 20TH JAN 1995. 9pm-6am
at THE RHYTHM STATION
STATION ROAD, ALDERSHOT, HAMPSHIRE

"AFTER BRINGING YOU ONE OF THE BEST PARTY'S OF LAST YEAR AT THE RHYTHM STATION WE'RE RETURNING ONCE AGAIN TO BRING YOU IN FULL EFFECT - OUR FIRST EVENT THIS YEAR. ONCE AGAIN WE'VE CONFIRMED A TOP QUALITY HAPPY HARDCORE DJ LINE-UP AS WELL AS 2 OF THE COUNTRY'S TOP PA'S - SLAMMIN' VINYL + KNITEFORCE - PLAYING BRAND NEW MATERIAL FOR 1995. IF YOU'RE ONE OF THE TRUE HARDCORE RAVERS WE'LL SEE YOU THERE!!!"

SLIPMATT – VIBES – ELLIS DEE
VINYLGROOVER - BRISK
RED ALERT - CUTT'N RUN
MC'S - ADRENALIN - MAGIKA

LIVE PA'S FROM SLAMMIN' VINYL + FUTURE PRIMITIVE FROM KNITEFORCE RECORDS

ATTRACTIONS: 100% MORE SOUND (DOUBLED AGAIN)
• MULTICOLOURED LAZERS • FULL LIGHTING
+ STROBE EFFECTS • LICENCED BAR + SECURE PARKING

HOUSE & GARAGE ALL NIGHT UPSTAIRS

INFORMATION HOT LINE - 0850 700983

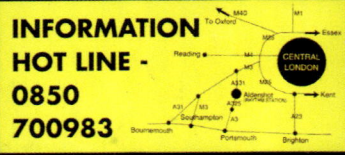

A FULL RANGE OF BRAND NEW MERCHANDISE IS AVAILABLE ON THE NIGHT AT AMAZING PRICES, SO BRING YOUR XMAS CASH !!!!

Pyramid Promotions presents

innersense

11th March
ARENA
LIVE PA BY "REMARC"
"RIP" & "Sound Murderer"
Randall
Mickey Finn
Probe & Brockie back2back
Ray Keith
Andy C
Swift
MC Flux, MC Dett
HOUSE ROOM
Mark Wright
Aphrodite
Bongo Man
Circuit
Arjaydee
Andy Lewis

18th March
ARENA
Grooverider
Dr S Gachet
Bryan Gee
Darren Jay
Kemistry & Storm
Andy C
NutEl
MC Fearless
MC Flux
HOUSE ROOM
Kenny Charles
Roger the Doctor
Circuit
Arjaydee
Andy Lewis

25th March
ARENA
Randall
Ray Keith
Fabio
DJ Rap
Probe
Flex
Marly Marl
MC Fats
MC Flux
HOUSE ROOM
John OOFleming
Rushmore presents
"Spirits of Inspiration"
Circuit
Arjaydee
Andy Lewis

8th April
ARENA
Mickey Finn
Hype
Grooverider
Ray Keith
Clarky
Probe
NutEl
MC Montana
MC Ragga Twins
HOUSE ROOM
Karisma
Operator
Circuit
Arjaydee
Andy Lewis

15th April
ARENA
Randall
Jumpin' Jack Frost
Grooverider
DJ Ron
Nikki Blackmarket
Dr S Gachet
Probe
HOUSE ROOM
hosted by
"Girls 106.8FM Night"
Kenny Charles
DJ Bird
Huckleberry Finn
Jacqui Manson
Rob Maynard

22nd April
ARENA
Randall
Ray Keith
Doc Scott
Darren Jay
DJ SS
DJ Rap
NutEl
HOUSE ROOM
Circuit
Arjaydee
Andy Lewis

For the 3rd sucessive year we thank all our members once again for voting us the "No.1 Best Club 1994."

1st April "UNIQUE ARTISTES NIGHT"
ARENA
Randall
DJ Ron
Brockie
Darren Jay
Andy C
Donovan Bad Boy Smith
Simon Bassline Smit
MC GQ
MC Flux & MC FiveO
HOUSE ROOM
Jesse
Neil
Circuit
Arjaydee
Andy Lewis

Easter Thursday 13th April "INNERSENSE DJ AWARDS 1995"
ARENA 1
Jumpin' Jack Frost
Grooverider
Mickey Finn
Brockie
Randall
Kenny Ken
Hype
Dr S Gachet
MC GQ
MC Dett

ARENA 2
Probe
DJ Ron
Tonic
Footloose
SL
Swift
Younghead
MC FiveO
MC Navigator

Tickets available in advance £16 (ticket includes £5 discount voucher for Innersense on 15th April 95.) £22 on the door.
See "INNERSENSE DJ AWARDS" flyer for outlets and further details.

ATTRACTIONS:-
Intelligent Light Show to blow your mind, includes 7 Watt multi coloured laser, 2 Golden Scans Mark3, 4 Intella Beams and much more. A 50k Sub bass breeze to let you know. Funky walkways. Ultra violet backdrops. Mobile circus. 16 TV Monitors.
SERVICES:-
Air Conditioning, Cloakroom, Snack Bar & Clean Toilets.
CLUB RULES:-
1. Walk through metal detector.
2. No mobile phones.
3. No drugs or alcohol.
4. No under 18s.
5. Right of admission reserved.

NO ADMISSION AFTER 1-30 AM ~ INFO LINE 0171 732 5047
INNERSENSE EVERY SATURDAY 10PM TO 7AM - £10 ADMISSION ON THE DOOR
LAZERDROME 267 RYE LANE, LONDON SE15

NEW YEAR'S EVE

31st December 1994

innersense

8pm to 7am

Innersense Promotion presents

Innersense is set to bring you the greatest New Years Eve celebration yet! Join us for the best in hardcore and jungle to the very end of '94 and bring '95 alive like never before. Innersense has always brought you the best. Get ready for better! Innersense '95.

We strongly recommend tickets are purchased in advance for our biggest party yet. Doors open at the earlier time of 8pm.

Be there!

Main Arena

Randall, Ray Keith, Grooverider, Fabio, Dr S Gachet, Hype Probe, Brockie, Nut E1

Live PA by
Renegade
' Terrorist' & ' Information Centre'
featuring Ray Keith & Nookie

Ultra violet performance by
Spectral Transmosis

plus
MC Reality & MC GQ

Chill-out

Kenny Charles, Roger the Doctor, Circuit, Arjaydee & Andy Lewis

Club Attractions

Multi-coloured Lazer, 50K Sub Bass Sound. Air Conditioning. Intelligent Lighting. Large Video Screen Projections. 16 TV Monitors. Multi Level Dance Platforms. Improved Chill-out sound system and carpet. Arcade Games, Snack Bar. Tight Polite Security.

24th Dec

Xmas Party

Main Arena

Krome.
Probe.
Randall,
Kenny Ken,
Ray Keith,
Dr S Gachet

Live PA by
Krome & Time
' The License' & ' Ganga Man'

Chill-out Guests
Operator
Spirits of Inspiration

£10 admission

Tickets...

£22 plus booking fee. Available in advance from the following outlets. (more on the door).
Tickets include £8 worth of discount vouchers for 7th and 14th January '95.

0233 629 706 Ashford/Richard Records	0494 436 426 High Wycombe/Buzz Records
0256 461 960 Basingstoke/Offbeat	081 547 0113 Kingston/Troublesome
0202 315 555 Bournemouth/M2	0622 757 859 Maidstone/Richard Records
0273 325 440 Brighton/Rounders	0843 231 333 Margate/Sonix
081 313 3413 Bromley/Blue Bird	0705 293 323 Portsmouth/Fusion
071 703 0501 Camberwell/New World Snooker	081 868 8637 Rayners Lane/Record Centre
0227 452 268 Canterbury/Richard Records	0734 573 922 Reading/Record Basement
0634 843 981 Chatham/Back to Back	0708 727 029 Romford/Boogie Times
071 351 6853 Chelsea/Section 5	0753 528 194 Slough/Record Centre
081 685 0708 Croydon/Wax City	071 494 0830 Soho/Unity
081 688 9627 Croydon/New World Snooker	071 437 0478 Soho/Blackmarket
0322 290 764 Dartford/Ard '2' Beats	0703 223 982 Southampton/Trip 2
081 568 6244 Ealing/Vinyl Mania	0702 436 893 Southend/Vinyl Rhythm
081 519 9882 Forest Gate/Underground	0831 127 981 Streatham/Mark
0474 321 931 Gravesend/Bitin' Back	081 885 2775 Tottenham/Just 4 The Beat
0483 451 002 Guildford, Dance 2 Records	0923 249 074 Watford/Freedom

Thanks to...

All the Lazerdrome staff, Scotts, Maria, Simon, Fish, Stanley, Lindsay, Noel, all the DJs that have played over the last year, Caroline (Unique Artists), Sarah & Lucy (Groove Connection), Alan (Kiss FM), Vernon (Don FM), Kool FM, John Peark, Gary Howard, The Saint Co, Weppens & Lisa, Dancers Sasha & Iesha, Final Touch 911 Security, Wingtight Security, Peter Cole, Peter & Randy, The Flying Squad, Turbo Terry (Scene Magazine), MC Reality, MC Whirlwinds, Jay (Atmosphere Magazine), Ultra Violet Task Force and finally thanks to you the ravers for all your faithful support.

Please note...

Strictly no admission after 1.30am, R.O.A.R. No alcohol. No illegal substances. No under 18's. **Please arrive early to avoid any disappointment.** Main Arena opens10pm **DOORS OPEN 8PM**

LAZERDROME 267 RYE LANE, LONDON SE15

LAZERDROME INFORMATION LINE: (071) 732 5047

Pyramid Promotions presents

innersense

Chill-out Residents every week
Circuit ~ Andy Lewis ~ Arjaydee

7th January
Clarky ~ NutEl ~ Cool Hand Flex ~ Dr S Gachet
Fabio ~ Ray Keith ~ DJ Rap ~
MC Reality ~ MC Flux
Chill-out Guests: Natasha ~ John 00 Fleming

14th January
Nikki Blackmarket ~ Andy C ~ Mickey Finn ~ Randall
Probe ~ Grooverider ~ MC Remadee ~ MC GQ
Chill-out Guests: Kenny Charles ~ Operator

21st January "BACK TO BACK"
DJ Ron 8B Brockie plus MC Dett
Jumpin' Jack Frost 8B Bryan Gee plus MC FiveO
Grooverider 8B Fabio plus MC Flux
Randall 8B Kenny Ken plus MC GQ
Chill-out Guests: Phil Asher ~ Rushmore

28th January
Mighty Marl ~ Darren Jay ~ Probe ~ Brockie ~
Dr S Gachet ~ NutEl ~ Hype ~
MC Dett ~ MC Reality
Chill-out Guests: Derek (Unity Records) ~
Roger the Doctor

4th February
Mampi Swift ~ Kemistry & Storm ~ Dr S Gachet ~
DJ Ron ~ LTJ Bukem ~ NutEl ~
MC Reality ~ MC FiveO
Chill-out Guests: Richie Fingers ~ Aphrodite

11th February "VALENTINE'S NIGHT"
11pm Fabio ~ 12.30am Andy C
2am Live PA by **DJ SS / ROLLERS CONVENTION**
2.30am Probe ~ 3.30am Mickey Finn ~
4.30am Grooverider ~ 5.30pm Randall
plus MC GQ ~ MC Moose
Chill-out: **"BACK TO THE SUMMER OF LOVE"**
10pm Nikki Blackmarket ~ 12am Phantasy ~
1.30am Jason Jay ~ 3.30am Rob Blake "The Marathon Man"
5am Roger the Doctor

18th February
NutEl ~ Darren Jay ~ Ray Keith ~ Hype
Dr S Gachet ~ Jumpin' Jack Frost ~
MC Reality ~ MC Flux
Chill-out Guests: Jumpin' Jack Frost ~ Matt Maurice

25th February
Clarky ~ Doc Scott ~ DJ Rap ~ Ray Keith ~ Randall ~
Grooverider ~ Probe ~ MC Remadee ~ MC Dett
Chill-out Guests: Tommy Cockles ~ Mickey B

ATTRACTIONS: Multicoloured Laser, 50K SubBass Sound, Air Conditioning, Intelligent Lighting, Large Video Screen
Projections, 16 TV Monitors, Dance Platforms, Snack Bar, Tight Polite Security.
PLEASE NOTE: Strictly no admission after 1.30am. R.O.A.R. No alcohol. No illegal substances. No under 18's.
Please arrive early to avoid disappointment. Doors open 10pm. Main Arena opens at 11pm.

INNERSENSE EVERY SATURDAY 10PM TO 7AM - £10 ADMISSION ON THE DOOR
LAZERDROME 267 RYE LANE, LONDON SE15
LAZERDROME INFORMATION LINE: (071) 732 5047

XMAS at the SCENE begins with

LUST

For people who love music, love dancing & above all love to look sexy, there is no other place to be but LUST.

SATURDAY DEC 19th
at THE SCENE
No 1 APPLETREE YARD SW1
10.30 till late

This is NOT repeat NOT for the faint hearted, are you ready for unrestricted LUST, we'll see!

2 different areas to dance, chill & be easy, balloons, free ice lollies, Santa's Grotto & ofcourse LUST music, the ultimate mixture of DANCE, GARAGE & FUNK as well as favourites guaranteed to please....yes I agree, far too much, for far to little!

PARTY TAX: £10 in advance (Guaranteed a place)
£10 on door (Limited number)

PRIZES

For the most raunchy & lustily clad male and female: £25 cash prize and a free hairdo at London's leading Salon Neville Daniel 25a Basil St. SW3 1BB SO REMEMBER, DRESS ACCORDINGLY AND WE'LL SEE YOU ON THE NIGHT!

TICKET INFO:
WITH EASE PROMOTIONS: 081 693 4798/0831 848488
THE SCENE: 071 839 5757

ONE NATION

"BEYOND THE DARKSIDE"

9 PM - 6 AM

£12

IN ADVANCE

ON SATURDAY 7TH MAY 1994
At Roller Express, Lea Valley Trading Estate
Angel Road, Edmonton, London N18

9 PM - 6 AM

£12

IN ADVANCE

THE MAIN ARENA

RANDALL · SWAN-E · RAP · HYPE
MARVELLOUS CAIN · PESHAY
DONOVAN 'BAD BOY' SMITH · DARREN JAY

ARENA TWO

PLAYING GARAGE · HOUSE · AND THE BEST OF THE OLD TUNES

ROB ANDREWS · HIGHLANDER · MOVE YA
MEDZ · SHAGGY MATT · MARC JAMES

ALL THIS IS 100% GUARANTEED SEE RAVESCENE AND ATMOSPHERE FOR FURTHER DETAILS!!

ATTRACTIONS TO MAKE YOUR FEEL FINE

50K PIRATE SOUND WITH EAW SUB-BASS · VIDEO SCREENS WITH LIVE EDITS · FULL LAZER AND
LIGHTING FX · EROTIC DANCERS · PEOPLE PLATFORMS · BRAIN MACHINES · VIDEO ARCADE
SECURE PARKING · CLOAKROOM AND PERSONAL LOCKERS · POLITE BUT TIGHT SECURITY
LICENSED BAR · HOT & COLD FOOD ALL NIGHT · FREE MINI BUS FROM TOTTENHAM HALE FROM
9 PM TO MIDNIGHT AND ABOVE ALL AN ATMOSPHERE GUARANTEED SECOND TO NONE

CREDIT CARD HOTLINE: 081 807 7345   **24 HOUR INFORMATION LINE: 081 887 0357**

TICKET OUTLETS & AGENTS
REGIONALS
Aldershot: Play It Again 0252 22155
Basingstoke: Off Beat Sports 0256 461960
Bournemouth: M2 Clothing 0202 315555
Brighton: Rounders Records 0273 25440
Camberley: Turbo Promotions 0276 686557
Eastbourne: Marlyn Music 0323 411832
Guildford: Dance 2 Records 0483 451002
High Wycombe: Buzz Records 0494 436426
Maidenhead: Hard Edge Records 0628 777797
Reading: Record basement 0734 573922

REGIONALS CONT
Slough: Record Centre 0753 528194
Slough: Ruff House 0753 551115
Southampton: T2 Records 0703 223982
Staines: Dancing Dog 0784 460397
Woking: Vinyl Frontier 0483 771413
Kent
Bexley Heath: Vinyl Conflict 081 298 1829
Bromley: Blue Bird Records 081 313 3413
Gravesend: Biting Back Records 0474 321931
Herne Bay: The White Label 0227 742691
Maidstone: Plastic Surgery Records 0622 661757

ESSEX
Basildon: (Lee) 0850 214141
Benfleet: Armageddon 0268 795668
Harlow: Pepe 0279 432270
Southend: Altered States 0374 610925
LONDON
Archway: Pure Groove 071 281 4877
Bethnal Green: Total Music 071 473 3000
Brixton: Global Explosion 071 652 3091
Camden: Zoom 071 267 4479
Central: Unity 071 734 2746
Croydon: Wax City 081 665 0708
Ealing: Vinyl Mania 081 566 5244

Edmonton: Roller Express 081 807 7345
Forest Gate: De Underground 081 519 9982
Hackney: Wired For Sound 081 985 7531
Haringay: Music Power 081 800 6113
Hounslow: Sugar Shack 081 569 6899
Ilford: Music Power 081 478 2080
Kingston: Troublesome 081 547 0113
Oxford Street: Razor 071 287 1695
Portabella Road: Pow Pow 081 969 0453
Rayners lane: Record Centre 081 868 8637
Soho: Black Market 071 437 0478
Tottenham: Just For The Beat 081 885 2775

ROAR · STRINGENT SEARCHES · NO ILLEGAL SUBSTANCES · BLAGGERS AND MOODY PEOPLE WILL NOT BE TOLERATED!
FLYING BY TURBO PROMOTIONS: 0276 686557

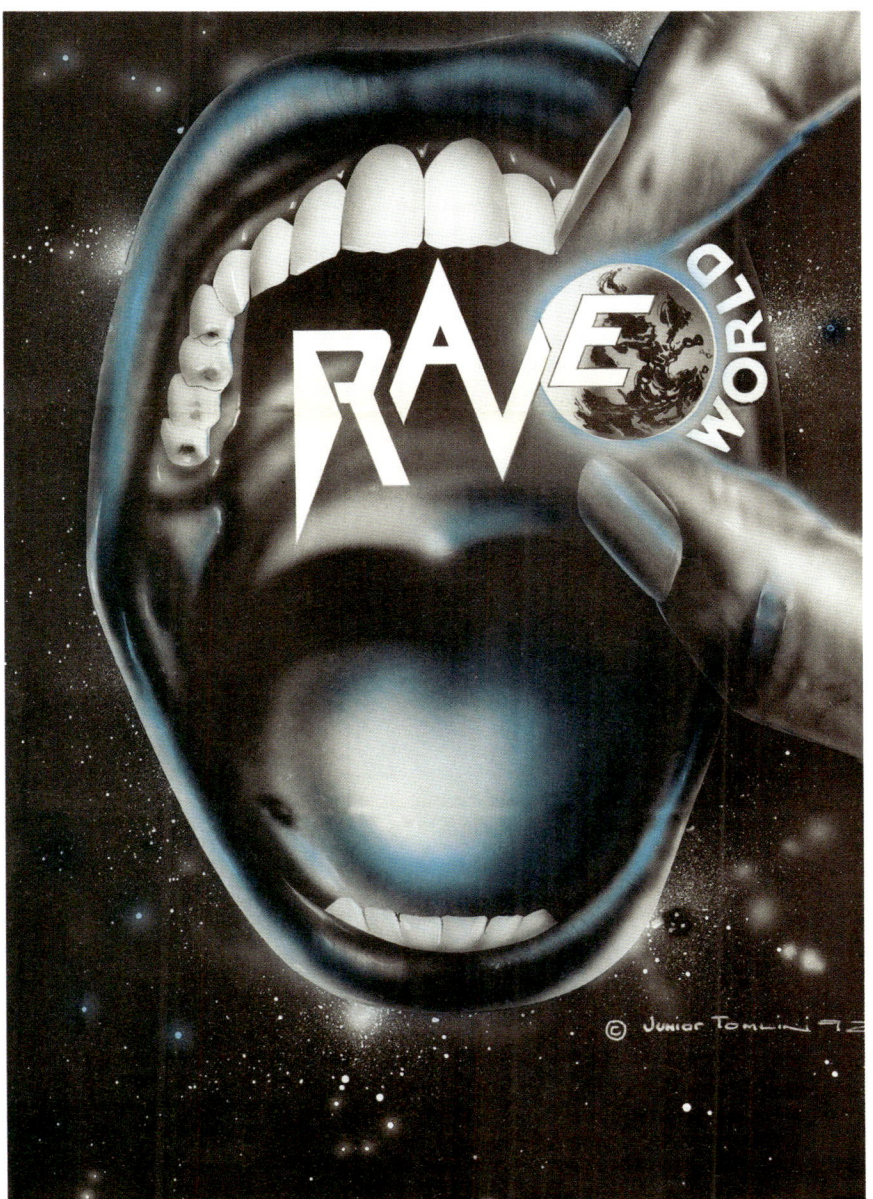

VENUE : LEAS CLIFF HALL, THE LEAS, FOLKSTONE, KENT

DATE : SATURDAY 18th JULY 1992 (HOTTEST DAY OF THE YEAR)

TIMES : 9 p.m. - 7 a.m. (ALL NIGHT LONG)

ONLY BUY YOUR TICKETS AT STATED OUTLETS / AGENTS

ATTRACTIONS

40 K PRO-SERIES SOUND RIG, 2 MULTI-COLOUR MIND BLOWING VISUAL SENSORY LAZERS, UV STROBES, GOLDEN SCANS, MASSIVE STAGGERED LEVEL DANCE FLATFORMS, FLAVOURED SMOKE, MULTI-COLOUR UV PAINTED BACKDROPS IN ABUNDANCE, STRANGE PROJECTIONS, EXTREMELY CRAZY COSTUMED DANCERS, ETC.

NECESSARIES

SECURE PARKING, METAL DETECTION, CONSCIENTIOUS SECURITY, FIRST AID, CLOAKROOM, SECURE TOILETS (CLEANED REGULARLY), JUICE BARS. THIS IS DEFINITELY ANOTHER SAFE VENUE.

PRODUCTION

AS THIS VENUE IS SIMILAR TO THE ASTORIA INSIDE, WE WILL UTILISE THE LARGE BALCONIES AND MASSIVE PILLARS AND HIGH CEILING TO THE FULLEST EFFECT POSSIBLE. YOU WILL NOT BE DISAPPOINTED, WE GUARANTEE IT.

FREEBIES

FLUORESCENT COLOURED WHISTLES, HORNS, MAD PUNCH (IN THE AIR) BALLS, SWEETS, STICKS OF ROCK, TOFFEE APPLES, AND TO REPLACE LOST VITAMIN C - A FRESH ORANGE FOR YOUR JOURNEY HOME, OR JUST SIT ON THE BEACH AND EAT IT AFTER.

TUFFDANCE & PLEASURE — NO POLITICS, JUST DANCE

A PERSONAL MESSAGE

WE HAVE CHECKED THE WEATHER FORECAST AND APPARENTLY THE 17th, 18th & 19th JULY ARE GOING TO BE THE HOTTEST DAYS OF THE YEAR SO BRING YOUR TOWELS BECAUSE WE WILL ALL BE GOING TO THE BEACH TO CHILL OUT AFTER - IT'S GONNA BE A HOT ONE.

STAY TUNED TO THESE STATIONS FOR UPDATES

KISS — 100 FM   SYNDICATE — 100.3 FM
TOUCHDOWN — 94 FM   PULSE — 90.6 FM

FUTURE EVENTS

WATCH OUT, BOURNEMOUTH, HARLOW, OXFORD & NORWICH - WE COULD BE COMING TO YOU VERY SOON!!!

RAVEWORLD PART III
☆ BAD INFLUENCE ☆

A DAY ARRIVES WHEN SOMETHING TAKES CONTROL OF YOU. IT MAKES YOU DO THINGS WHICH YOU MIGHT NOT HAVE USUALLY DONE. YOU START STAYING OUT ALL NIGHT, TRAVELLING MANY MILES WITH OTHERS WHO FEEL THE SAME WAY AS YOU. YOU DANCE FOR HOURS AND HOURS IN YOUR OWN WORLD. NOT KNOWING THE REALITY OF TIME. YOU ESCAPE FROM THE PROBLEMS AND HORRORS OF THE REAL WORLD, YOU BECOME ONE WITH ALL AROUND YOU, BUT WHEN YOU TRY TO EXPLAIN TO OTHERS WHO DON'T THINK THE SAME WAY AS YOU, ALL THEY SAY IS YOU'RE JUST UNDER A *BAD INFLUENCE.*

DJ's SUPPLYING THE INFLUENCE

COLIN DALE	ELLIS DEE	L T J BUKEM
RANDALL	ROCK	VIBES
PHYSICS	DEVIOUS D	PESHAY

WARNING : DJ's WILL NOT BE PLAYING ANY RECORD BELOW 125 BPM

RAVEWORLD : ATTRACTING THINKING, RESPONSIBLE, RAVERS

THE ULTIMATE CHILL-OUT
WATCH THE SUN RISE OVER THE SEA TO THE MUSIC OF THESE RISING STARS

DJ BARRETT	KRS	DANNY C
WARLOCK	SPIRIT CHILD	DJ DANCE
MR BENN	JBL	BUZBY	JASON B

RAVEWORLD : EXPLORING DEEP BODY PLEASURE

THE BEST NEW P.A. ON THE CIRCUIT - BACK BY DEMAND
D.E.A — GOLD CHILL
(LIVE SCRATCHING BY DEVIOUS D)

MC's TO KEEP THE MOOD RIGHT ALL NIGHT !
J. SLY (DEA)
REMO DON (KICKIN)

SPECIAL GUEST
MR 3-D. THE ULTIMATE BOTTOM PINCHING RAVER FRIENDLY ROBOT WILL BE APPEARING WITH HIS BUCKET AND SPADE.

RAVEWORLD : AFFECTING YOUR MIND

TICKETS

TICKETS ARE £12 IN ADVANCE + 10% BOOKING FEE. THESE ARE AVAILABLE WITH THE AGENTS & OUTLETS LISTED BELOW.
A CERTAIN AMOUNT OF TICKETS WILL BE HELD BACK FOR THE NIGHT PRICED AT £15.
WE STRONGLY ADVISE YOU TO PURCHASE YOUR TICKETS IN ADVANCE TO GUARANTEE YOUR ENTRY ON ARRIVAL. THERE WILL BE A SEPARATE FAST ENTRY SYSTEM FOR ADVANCE TICKET HOLDERS.

TICKET OUTLETS & AGENTS

KENT OUTLETS
Richards Records (Ashford) - 0233 629706
Richards Records (Canterbury) - 0227 452626
Hummingbird (Dover) - 0304 202328
Hummingbird (Folkstone) - 0303 43636
Hummingbird (Ramsgate) - 0843 590750
Richards Records (Maidstone) - 0622 757868
Compact Disc (Seven Oaks) - 0732 740688
Sitting Duck (Gravesend) - 0474 321801
Record Centre (Margate) - 0753 526494

ESSEX OUTLETS
Boogie Times (Romford) - 0708 727025
World Class Records (Colchester) - 0206 768876
Soul Man (Southend) - 0702 355444
Skipped Disc (Billericay) - 0277 631422
Dance Juice (Brentwood) - 0277 201102
Rex Records (Ipswich) - 0473 234819
Compost (Basildon) - 0268 286979

LONDON OUTLETS
Zoom (London) - 071 267 4479
Music Power (Ilford) - 081 478 3580
Blast For Sound (Hackney) - 081 985 1931
Dance Floor (Finsbury, SW18) - 081 673 5575
Unity Records (New St, W1) - 071 734 7766
Vinyl Mania (W Ealing) - 081 566 6244
De Underground (Forest Gate) - 081 519 9982
Rare Shop (Wandsworth) - 081 965 7766

REGIONAL OUTLETS
Jelly Jam (Brighton) - 0273 75026
Primadonna (Cambridge) - 1233 350225
Soul Sense (Luton) - 0582 25337
Catmate (Bournemouth - 0202 547 793
Steve Jason (Peterborough) 0733 555 75

TICKET AGENTS

Pleasure Promotions
Rob, Mario (Essex) - 0836 764692
                     0706 795382
(Scott) (East London) - 061 530 2438
(Candice) (South London) - 071 738 4520
Danny (West London - 0831 470 364
Moxine (Brighton - 0273 27957
                    0860 606244
Warren (Folkestone - 0233 626722
Darren (Gravesend) - 0474 632990
Justin (Braintree) - 0371 356773

TUFFDANCE & PLEASURE PROMOTIONS INFO LINES
0206 795382   0206 735735
0836 264692   0831 478354
081 530 2435   071 738 4520

CREDIT CARD HOLDERS — 0735 60075

MAIN APPROACH ROADS
A TO Z Gt Britain Road Atlas P21 P198 & P267

WE ARE HERE

SEND US YOUR NAME & ADDRESS FOR FUTURE MAIL OUTS
OUR MAILING ADDRESS IS: 82 HERMYWER ROAD, LONDON E13 9HN

MERCHANDISE RANGES OF RAVEWORLD II AND DEVERS III AT RAVEWORLD AND MEMBERSHIP WILL
SOON BE AVAILABLE, MAKE SURE WE HAVE YOUR NAME & ADDRESS.

CREDITS — Original Artwork - Junior Tomlin —
              Flyer Design & Layout - Kerry Monster
              Acts, DJs & PAs – Tuffdance

NO NO's —
              No illegal substances, no under 18's (sorry), no lightweights.
              R.O.A.R, S.N.A. Searches on Entry & Venue Approaches.

RAVE WORLD
* THE ULTIMATE IN RAVE EXPERIENCE *

TUFFDANCE AND KICKIN PROMOTIONS HAVE JOINED FORCES
AND COMBINED RESOURCES TO TAKE YOU TO A HIGHER PLAIN
IN A NEW DIMENSION OF RAVE EXPERIENCE!

PREPARE TO BE MUSICALLY ENLIGHTENED A S YOU ARE NOW
ABOUT TO DISCOVER A NEW FEVER PITCH HIGH IN THE
UTOPIAN WORLD OF RAVE!

PREPARE TO WITNESS THE AWESOME POWER OF RAVE WORLD!

THE ULTIMATE DJ LINE UP FOR THE HARDCORE!

DEVIOUS D	PHYSICS
L.T.J. BUKEM	RANDALL
LOFT GROOVER	ELLIS DEE
SIMON 'BASSLINE' SMITH	SWANN 'E'

WARNING — ANY RECORD BELOW 125 BPM WILL NOT BE PLAYED

A 2ND ROOM FOR THE HARDCORE (SORRY NO GARAGE)

PESHAY, A TO Z, T.K.O., THE JINX, JBL,
BUZBY, D.J. DEX, SPIRIT CHILD, MR BENN

WATCH OUT FOR THESE NAMES IN THE FUTURE

NOTHING WILL BE LEFT TO CHANCE!

★ MADNESS WILL REIGN AT RAVE WORLD! ★

THE TWO MOST EXCITING P.A.'s TO HIT THE RAVE WORLD

D.E.A. — THEIR LAST P.A. CAUSED A STAGE INVASION

WISHDOKTA — BEWARE OF THE FLYING BANANAS.
YOU HAVE BEEN WARNED

THE ABOVE P.A.'s WERE PICKED BECAUSE OF THEIR ORIGINAL PRODUCTIONS

THREE MC's TO BEND THOSE KNEES

JAY JAY (SL11)   J. SLY (D.E.A.)   L.J. ROCK

WARNING: MC's WILL ONLY PERFORM FOR 10 MINS EACH HOUR

**DON'T JUST GET TO HEAR ABOUT IT!
BE THERE TO SEE IT!!**

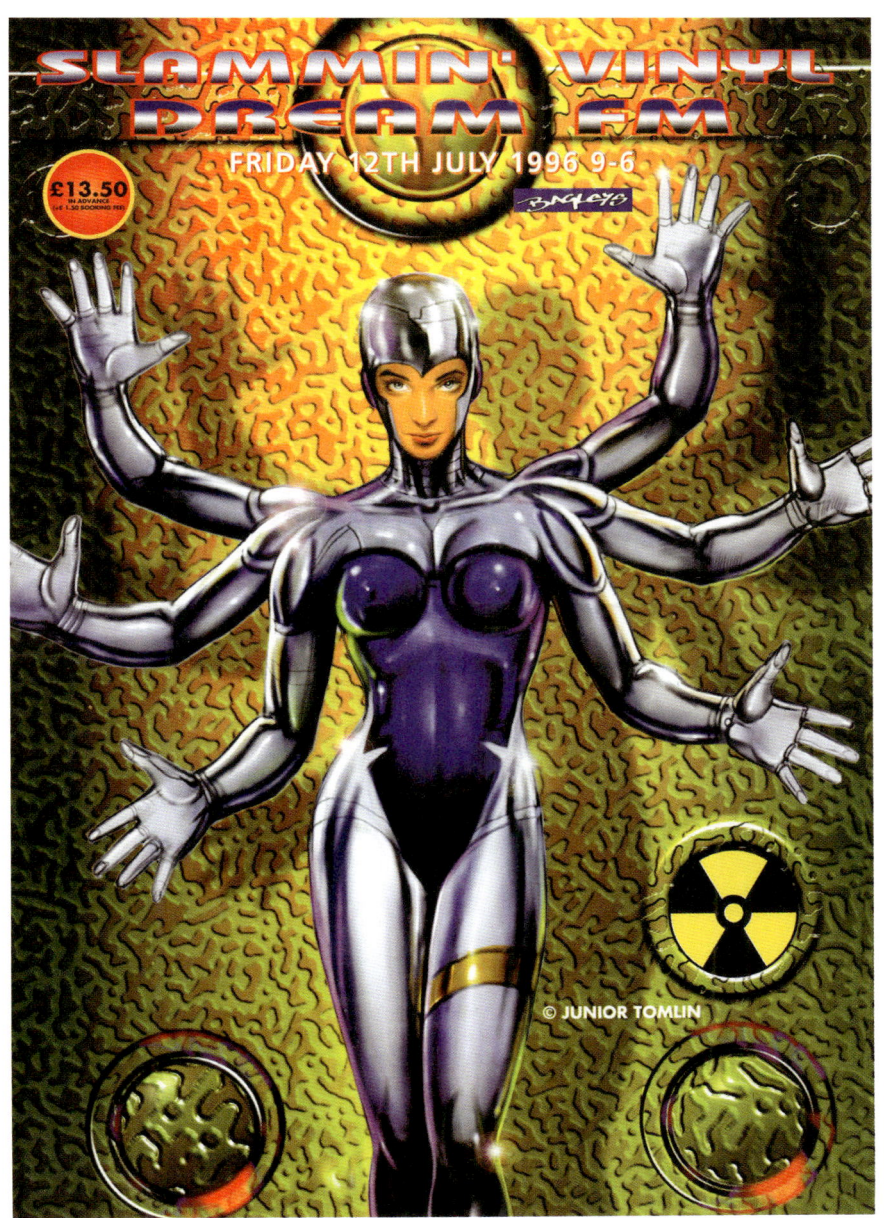

FRIDAY 12th JULY 9-6

BAGLEYS FILM STUDIOS
YORK WAY, KINGS CROSS, LONDON (OFF GOODSWAY)

£13.50

WE GUARANTEE TO BRING YOU THE LARGEST HARDCORE EVENT IN LONDON THIS SUMMER. SLAMMIN' VINYL AND DREAM FM HAVE NOW ESTABLISHED OURSELVES AS THE CAPITAL'S LEADING HARDCORE PROMOTERS AFTER THE SUCCESS OF OUR FIRST THREE EVENTS THIS YEAR. IN OUR SUMMER SPECTACULAR WE WILL AGAIN EXPAND BAGLEYS TO INCLUDE YET ANOTHER ARENA BRINGING YOU: THE FINEST HAPPY HARDCORE, DRUM & BASS AND HOUSE & GARAGE. ALL THIS FOR AN UNBEATABLE PRICE OF £13.50 WHICH OTHER PROMOTERS CANNOT MATCH. BELIEVE THE HYPE AND MAKE SURE YOU'RE THERE!!!

ARENA 1
SLIPMATT
GROOVERIDER
SY + UNKNOWN
HYPE
JIMMY J
SEDUCTION
SPINBACK
ENERGY
INFLUENCE
TOM THUMB
MC'S
GQ, MAGIKA, RUFF

ARENA 2
DOUGAL
VIBES
RANDALL
SLAM
KENNY KEN
MIXTER
UPROAR
DOUBLE D
DESIRE
WISE
MCS
SHARKY, TWILIGHT
SUICIDE

ARENA 3
HOUSE & GARAGE
NANCY NOISE
(LEISURE LOUNGE)
ROY THE ROACH
(KISS 100 FM)
NICK DARE
(CLUB UK)
DAVE & STUART
(BRM)
CHARLIE BROWN
ANDY FORD
GUSSY

50 K OF F2 TURBO SOUND, 2X MULTICOLOURED LASER SYSTEMS, STATE OF THE ART LIGHTING, DANCE PLATFORMS, INFLATABLES, MASSIVE OUTDOOR CHILLOUT AREA, MERCHANDISE STAND, LICENSED BAR, MASSIVE VIDEO PROJECTION SCREENS, SONY PLAYSTATION AREA, GYROSCOPE, FACE PAINTING, ARENA 4 (FORMALLY ARENA 5) WILL BE A CHILLOUT AREA SECURITY PATROLLED CAR PARKS AND A SAFE AND ATTITUDE FREE EVENT, NEW FRIENDLY SECURITY WITH IMPROVED QUEUEING TO ENSURE FAST ENTRY, OVER 18'S PLEASE BRING ID

CREDIT CARD LINES
INFO LINES: 0171 344 4444
0181 780 083
0181 547 9113
0171 387 2208
0181 299 344
0171 978 0771

DREAM FM 107.6

OR VISIT THE SLAMMIN' VINYL SHOPS APPLE RECORDS, KINGSTON UPON THAMES. DON'T GUARANTEED BUY TICKETS EARLY AS THIS IS A GUARANTEED SELLOUT AGAIN!!!

DESIGN & LAYOUT & IMAGES © JUNIOR TOMLIN

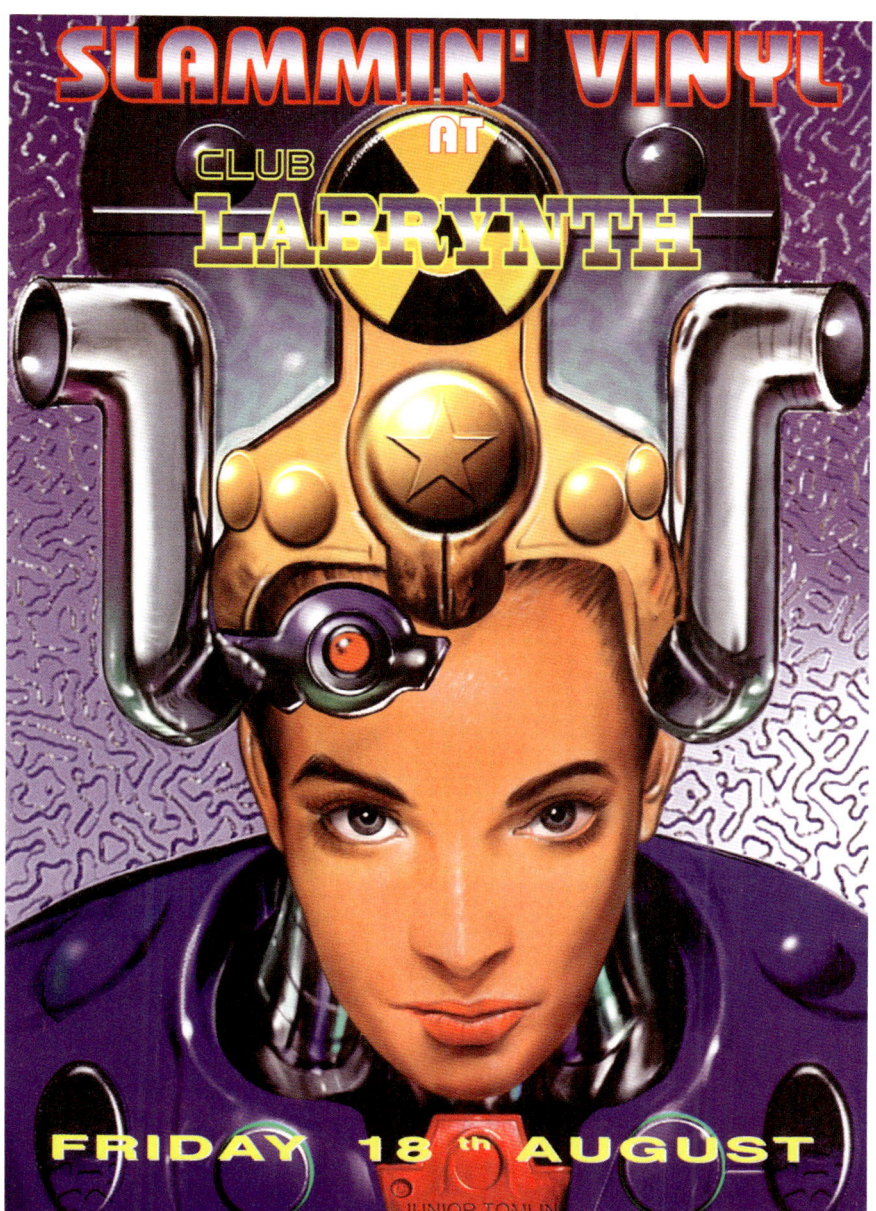

£10 ON THE DOOR

£8 MEMBERS

SLAMMIN' VINYL
AT
CLUB
LABRYNTH

FRIDAY 18th AUGUST 11- 6 AM
12 DALSTON LANE, LONDON E 8

SLAMMIN' VINYL RETURNS TO LONDON TOUCHING DOWN AT THE LEGENDARY CLUB LABRYNTH, TRANSFORMING THIS VENUE WITH A MASSIVE D,J LINE UP, AN AMAZING LIGHT SHOW INCLUDING A 10 WATT MULTICOLOURED LAZER & A STUNNING UV BACKDROP DISPLAY. AS ALWAYS NO BAD ATTITUDE IS TOLERATED SO ONLY THE HAPPIEST OF PEOPLE NEED APPLY

SEDUCTION - SY - VIBES
RED ALERT - SLAM
BILLY BUNTER - JIMMY J

BASEMENT
MATT MAURICE
STEVIE BRINN
EASY MO

ATTIC
REMIX RECORDS CREW
RICHIE B
COLIN GEORGE
DJ DESIRE

10 WATT MULTICOLOURED LAZER SAFE PARKING WITH SECURITY CHECKS
ROBOSCANS, ROBO ZAPS + FULL UV FX BRAND NEW UV. BACKDROPS

INFO LINES
0850 700983
0171 247 0789

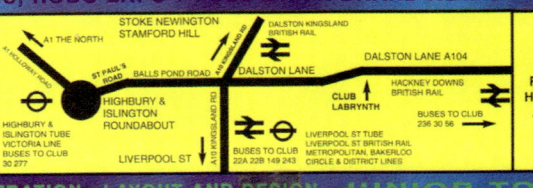

FULL RANGE OF MERCHANDISE RECORDS, WHISTLES HORNS ETC, FOR SALE AT BARGAIN PRICES

ILLUSTRATION , LAYOUT AND DESIGN   JUNIOR TOMLIN

The Awakening

£10 adv. + £1 booking
£12.50 on the door
early ticket purchase
ensures entry
Credit card hotline
0271 74447

Your M.C.s for the night

JACK HORNER

MUSCLE HEAD

SQUIDGY B

PROUDLY PRESENT AT
THE WAREHOUSE UNION STREET PLYMOUTH
FRIDAY 9TH APRIL 1993 8PM – 2AM

MAIN ARENA CONTRACTED D.J.s IN ORDER OF APPEARANCE
SCORPIO The S.W. finest up n' coming PHANTASY Fantazia Raindance Perception Just back from dates in Oz & Canada
SWAN E Fantazia vision dreamscape COLIN DALE The Knowledge Club Kiss F.M.s top international DJ in
Plymouth for the 1st time EASYGROOVE THE ORIGINAL TECHNODREDD Universe fantazia Obsession The World!
ARENA TWO BEN McGOWAN Soundz Positivity EASYGROOVE Wicked Wicked fluffy set MATT PERRY Mighty Force
ATTRACTIONS Lazer Robots A most humongous sound system with enough bass to blow
your head off Wicked lighting and multi – coloured lasers by Fineline of Bristol:The
Business!! The Children of Kaos will complete the enhancement of your environment with
an awesome inner skin and superb F.X.

The words out; Plymouth's buzzin' again and OMNITECH are proud to be back at the Warehouse,
the S.W.'s top dance venue. We have assembled some of the U.K.'s finest D.J.'s & M.C.'s together
with 1st class production crews to bring you THE AWAKENING. Come and be part of it!!

FULLY LICENSED BARS OVER 18'S ONLY R.O.A.R. NO ILLEGAL SUBSTANCES SEARCHES ON ENTRY ALL ATTRACTIONS CONTRACTED-
SECURITY COURTESY OF MILLIE ROSE LTD. IN CONJUNTION WITH McDONNELL SECURITY – VERY TIGHT BUT VERY POLITE
FLYER DESIGN BY DAVY AT A WAVE GRAPHIC 0803 298634

OMNITECH OFFICIAL OUTLETS PLEASE BUY ONLY FROM OFFICIAL OUTLETS TO AVOID FORGERIES
COACH / TICKET / & INFO LINES : PORTSMOUTH/SO'TO'N/ BOURNEMOUTH/WEYMOUTH/DORCHESTER
CAMIE / SARAH 0202 547250   NORTH DEVON/ C ORNWALL CONCERT TRAVEL 0271 74447 10 LINES

BARNSTAPLE	UP FRONT	0271 74187	PENZANCE	SOUND CHECK	0736 60429
BODMIN	SOUNDS	0208 78722	PLYMOUTH	MUSIC BOX	0752 361920
BOURNMOUTH	WILD THINGS	0202 315873	PLYMOUTH	RIVAL	0752 221952
BRIDGEWATER	WEST QUAY	0278 428509	PORTSMOUTH	JELLYJAM	0705 877947
BRISTOL	TRIBE OF ONE	0272 225200	ST AUSTELL	SAFFRON	0726 75071
BUDE	UP BEAT	0288 355763	SO'THAMPTON	MOVEMENT REC'DS	0703 211333
DORCHESTER	RECORD CENTRE	0305 266511	TAUNTON	SOUND CHECK	0823 321385
EXETER	MIGHTY FORCE	0392 433844	TORQUAY	IDENTITY	0803 214368
EXETER	ROCKAFELLAS	0392 422355	TORQUAY	SOUNDZ	0803 211097
EXMOUTH	NANDA DEVI	0395 278149	TRURO	OPUS MUSIC	0872 223327
FALMOUTH	COMPACT RECORD	0326 311936	WADEBRIDGE	RECORD SELECT	0208 812625
NEWQUAY	CRIMINAL RECORD	0637 851564	WEYMOUTH	TOTALLY U'D'RGND	0305 761609
PAIGNTON	SOUNDZ	0803 556893	YEOVIL	ACORN RECORDS	0935 25503

ENTROPY PROMOTIONS
in association with
LEGENDARY
presents

DANCE NATION
BANK HOLIDAY DANCE SPECTACULAR

at
SPEEDKARTING, WARRINGTON, CHESHIRE
(100,000 sq.ft. INDOOR WAREHOUSE)
COMMENCES: SUNDAY 24th MAY 11pm-7am BANK HOLIDAY MONDAY 25th MAY 1992
THE LARGEST ALL NIGHT LICENSE EVER TO BE GRANTED IN THE NORTH
NO OTHER EVENT ON THIS NIGHT WILL COMPARE IN SIZE OR QUALITY

*** ENTROPY *** LEGENDS ***

Jointly Presents
*** LEGENDARY III ***
As One

DANCE NATION

ALL NIGHT · BANK HOLIDAY DANCE SPECTACULAR · ALL NIGHT

GATES OPEN SUNDAY 24th MAY 10.00pm · 7.00am BANK HOLIDAY MONDAY 25th MAY at

SPEEDKARTING, WARRINGTON, CHESHIRE
(100,000 sq.ft. indoor warehouse, just off the M6, Junction 20. Follow AA Signs for the event)

INTRODUCTION

It is often said that the best things come to those who wait. Well, we are pleased to announce that the wait is over. People from all over the country will gather to attend the largest Legal all night party ever in the North of England. No other event in the area has ever featured such a high standard of production to compliment the U.K.'s finest selection of D.J.'s. **REMEMBER.... This is where the atmosphere is. DON'T MISS IT!!!**

THE U.K.'s FINEST D.J.'s

CARL COX □ STU ALLAN □ TOP BUZZ □ GROOVERIDER □ DAZ WILLOT □
□ MIKE WOODS □ EASY GROOVE/LISA □ DJ RAPP □ NOGGY □

ATTRACTIONS

□ 100,000 sq.ft. Dance Area □ 75K of Pure Sub Bass □ Dance Platforms In All The Right Places □
□ Dance Nation — Dance Squad □ Multi Coloured laser Display - 3 Seperate Systems □ Laser Robot □
□ Laser Dancers □ Gyroscopes □ Complete Visual Stage Show □ Velcro Wall □ Various Outdoor Stalls □
□ Rodeo Bull □ The Whole Venue Will Be Packed With Lighting Effects To Produce The Ultimate Visual Show □
□ Food And Soft Drinks Bar □ Ample Toilet Facilities □ Cloakroom □ Information Desk □

LIVE P.A.

MAN PARRIS # SHADES OF RHYTHM **LETHAL MC**

TICKET OUTLETS / AGENTS

TICKETS ON SALE NOW.

 **ENJOY** EST 1991

ENJOY PRODUCTION PRESENTS

DIMENSION X

Thursday 16th January 1992

FOR THOSE WHO KNOW - WATCH THIS SPACE

DECK TECHNICIANS ON THE NIGHT

V I P & DOVE • **DJ SAM** • **THE GODFATHER**
(THE FOG . ENJOY)   (HELTER SKELTER)   (DUNGEONS . WONDERLAND)

ELLIS DEE • **PHANTASY** • **FRANKIE BONES**
(PERCEPTION . RAINDANCE)   (TIME . STARLIGHT)   (BEYOND THERAPY)

MC PADDY DE

FOR YOUR PLEASURE

12K TURBO SOUND . TERRA STROBES . ZIP ARCHLINE . UV CANNONS
10 KVA OPTIKENITIC LIGHTING RIG . ROBO ZAPS . ROBO SKANS
ARGON AIR COOLED LAZER BUBBLE MACHINE . THE FOG . MAD BACKDROPS

NEED WE SAY MORE ? WE GUARANTEE YOUR RETURN
YOUR PROMISED A TOTALLY TRANSFORMED VENUE AS NEVER SEEN BEFORE

TAKING PLACE AT

9pm - 5am **MILLWAUKEES** **9pm - 5am**

ON THE A6 BETWEEN RUSHTEN AND BEDFORD (SOULDROP TURN)
● PLEASE ARRIVE EARLY TO AVOID DISAPPOINTMENT ●

NO ILLEGAL SUBSTANCES
STRINGENT SEARCHES ON
ENTRY

£6.00

MILLWAUKEES BOX OFFICE 0234 781610
ENJOY PRODUCTION (ALEX) 0933 228882

WE ENJOY WOULD LIKE TO THANK 'YOU' FOR ROCKIN THE FOG 91
"ENJOY" AND WELCOME TO 92

FRE
EDO
M

FREEDOM

That's What Life's About

27th MARCH SATURDAY 1993

THE
PYRAMID WAREHOUSE
ASHWIN STREET, LONDON E8

ANOMIE PRODUCTIONS PRESENTS 10.00pm – 7.00am

THAT'S
WHAT
LIFES
ABOUT
ESTABLISHED 1989

FREEDOM

THAT'S
WHAT
LIFES
ABOUT
ESTABLISHED 1989

"RETURN OF THE HARDCORE"

TO BE STAGED AT THE

THE PYRAMID WAREHOUSE

ASHWIN STREET LONDON E.8
OFF KINGSLAND HIGH STREET
(Map on tickets)

TICKETS £10.00 more on the door

TO BE INCLUDED ON THE MAILING LIST PLEASE
SEND TO: ANOMIE PRODUCTIONS, THE
GORDON AGENCY, 198 HIGH RD. LONDON N22

NAME ....
ADDRESS..
....
DOB ....

SATURDAY 27th MARCH 1993

As promised Freedom entered 1993 on a *Top Buzz*. We apologize to the hundreds that couldn't get in. For those that made it in... you know the atmosphere was electric! We know you were buzzing to the *maxium*. It was a tremendous evening – we aim to continue the vibe throughout this year. A big *respect* goes out to you. 1993 is ours and freedom will take you all the way. We're going to tear the *roof down*! PEACE!

Design & Artwork Craig.E-Mac's 071-354 1996

ARENA 1
"HARDCORE COMPOSERS"
GROOVE RIDER ✦ DONAVON (BADBOY) SMITH ✦ SWANN-E
✦ ASLAM MAC ✦ TORCHMAN ✦ RANDALL ✦ THE RED ANT

MC ANOMIE ✳ MC RUFF ✳ BONE-MAN-X ✳ MC HYDRO

These MC's are proper rave MC's not MC's who give shouts to their mates all nite. These MC's are selected to create the hype necessary to give a kickin atmosphere

ATTRACTIONS   ARENA 2

✦ 35K TURBO SOUND SYSTEM ✦
2 MULTICOLOURED LASERS ✦
LASERROBOTS ✦ PROJECTIONAL
ROTATING CUBE ✦ UV ART ✦
GYROSCOPES ✦ DANCE PLATFORMS
✦YOU CAN BET YOUR ASS THAT THE
FREEDOM PRODUCTION WILL BE
KICKIN. ENOUGH LIGHTS AND
LASERS TO BLOW YOU AWAY.

"NEW KIDS ON THE BLOCK"
VIBES ✦ BATCH ✦ ROB FOSTER ✦ NOODLES

Ask any DJ today how hard it is to get a chance to "BREAK THROUGH" and play at a respected rave organization party. The DJ's above have been chosen because they are the DJ's of tomorrow.

TO HEAR THE HYPE! 0831 824 400

TICKET OUTLETS

HYPERBOLIC
FRIDAY 20TH MAY
8PM TIL 6AM

HYPERBOLIC

FRIDAY 20TH MAY
8PM TILL 6AM
THE SPEEDWAY STADIUM
SADDLEBOW RD KINGS LYNN

AFTER THE SUCCESS OF OUR LAST TWO EVENTS WE ARE PROUD
TO ANNOUNCE MONTHLY EVENTS AFTER MAY BRINGING YOU
THE FAMOUS HYPERBOLIC BUZZ RESPECT TO ALL THOSE PEOPLE
WHO HAVE SUPPORTED US WE WILL BRING YOU THE BEST
ALLNIGHT PARTY'S MONEY CAN BUY

TWO ROOMS OF MUSIC

FOR THE HARDCORE MASSES
BRINGING BACK THE FUN

DJ FREE FALL ~ STEVE K
DJ DYNAMIX
DJ DANCE
DJ UNITY
RANDALL
DOUGAL
GROOVE RIDER

MCS SCREETCH INFINITY HAVOC

PLUS THE WIDELY RENOWNED
HOUSE ROOM
THE RHYTHM SECTION
STEVE K ~ PAUL GRANT ~ PEE WEE

ATTRACTIONS
10K MARTIN A5S SOUND
SUPPLIED BY SABIQ 0553 841968
3 LASER SYSTEMS
SUPPLIED BY K TRAX 0406 365005
UV BACKDROPS SUPPLIED BY BANARAMA

ADMISSION £10 B4 1 O'CLOCK
FOR MAILING LIST & FURTHER INFO CALL
0374 220712 0553 770843
0406 365005

THE ESSENTIAL EXPERIENCE

FRIDAY 3RD DECEMBER 1993 THE WAREHOUSE UNION STREET PLYMOUTH 7.30PM-2.00AM

THE NAUGHTY BOYS ARE BACK! THE PEOPLE WHO BROUGHT YOU THE "ULTIMATE PARTY NIGHT" RETURN WITH WHAT WILL BE THE LAST HARDCORE EVENT TO BE HELD AT THE WAREHOUSE THIS YEAR. THE OMNITECH PRODUCTION CREW WILL SURPASS ALL PREVIOUS EVENTS WITH A FULL LASER AND INTELLIGENT LIGHT SHOW PLUS STROBES, FLAVOURED SMOKE AND TWO OUTRAGEOUSLY ENORMOUS SOUND RIGS TO ENSURE THE USUAL OMNITECH BASS LINE THAT LITERALLY ROCKS THE PLACE! IN ADDITION, TWO HUGE PROJECTION SCREENS WILL DOMINATE THE STAGE WITH AMAZING ANIMATED AND COMPUTER GENERATED IMAGES. FINALLY, THE CHILDREN OF KAOS WILL PROVIDE ANOTHER OUTSTANDING STAGE SET AND INNER SKIN TO SET THE SCENE FOR WHAT WILL UNDOUBTEDLY BE AN ESSENTIAL EXPERIENCE. BE THERE PILGRIMS: WE WONT LET YOU DOWN!!

THE MAIN ARENA

7.30-8.30 D.J. WORM
PANDEMONIUM, FANTAZIA,
THE SOUTH WEST D.J. MAKES A WELCOME
RETURN TO THE WAREHOUSE.

8.30-10. LOFTGROOVER
ABSOLUTELY NO INTRO NEEDED -
LOFTGROOVER STEPS UP EARLY TO BRING
YOU THE KNOWLEDGE!

10-11 SCORPIO
ARGUABLY THE S.W. TOP D.J., SCORPIO
HAS RECENTLY BEEN ROCKIN'
REVELATION AND KAOS AND WILL BE
PLAYIN' KNOWLEDGE ON 12/1/94

11-12 COLIN DALE
THE MADMAN RETURNS!
OBSESSION, UNIVERSE, KISS F.M.
HELLRAISER (HOLLAND) ENERGETIC
(SWITZERLAND) MAYDAY (GERMANY)

12-1 TREVOR ROCKLIFFE
AFTER HIS AWESOME SET AT "THE
ULTIMATE PARTY NIGHT" TREVOR WILL
AGAIN ROCK THE WAREHOUSE WITH HIS
WICKED 3 DECK MIX OF HARDHOUSE AND
TECHNO

1-2 STU ALLAN
OBSESSION, DANCE PLANET, UNIVERSE,
THE EDGE, KINETIC QUEST & JUST ABOUT
EVERYWHERE REALLY! STANDBY FOR
ACTION & SOME SUPERB MIXING FROM STU
WHO IS MANCHESTER KEY PICCADILLY
103FM'S FINEST DANCE D.J.

FOLLOWING THEIR MOST
EXCELLENT SHOW AT THE
"ULTIMATE PARTY NIGHT"
PLYMOUTHS' VERY OWN
CULTURAL VIBES CREW
WILL AGAIN BE ROCKING
THE CHILL OUT WITH THE
STYLE OF HAPPY HOUSE
THAT HAS SEEN THEIR
EXCELLENT SATURDAY
CLUB NIGHT ROCKET TO #5
IN D.J. MAGAZINES'
NATIONAL CLUB-CHART.
PARTY ANIMALS ON THE
NIGHT ARE VERDÉ, PHIL
BUBB, DUNCAN PARKS,
BEN McGOWAN AND
HUGH JANUS -- MAD!!

SHOUTS 2; Mr Troy and the Girlies, Carl, Rachel, and the Dudes at Ultimate. Roger, Sean, Phil and the Warehouse Crew, Fineline of Bristol, Sonix Concert Systems, The Children of Kaos, Frantic Fractals, To everyone who created the Wicked vibe at "the Ultimate Party Night" and to the whole South West Party - Massive

WHATYOUSEE IS WHATYOUGET WITH OMNITECH - AND THEN SOME

ALL NIGHT **ZILLION** PHASE 1 **ALL NIGHT**

SATURDAY 15TH JUNE 1991

ZILLION

PHASE 1

S A T U R D A Y   1 5 T H   J U N E   1 9 9 1

The joined forces of the top UK event organisations of 89/90 bring you the PREMIER of their 1991 events, Zillion, Phase 1. Linking a top National line up of DJ's and PA's, never before seen live, all on the same stage. This Multi-Media event will boast an entirely new concept in world sounds, with enough lights, lazers and optic fibre to take you into cyberspace, featuring the first ever showing of Zillions unique Lazer Webb and Virtual Reality Simulator giving you the ultimate all night dance experience.

TRUE DEX MASTERS

West Country's **EASY GROOVE** (Perception)	North England's top DJ **SASHA** Amnesia - Shelly's - Hacienda	Midlands DJ **MICKY FINN** Amnesia - Eclipse Coventry	South Coast DJ **AUBREY** Sterns - Astoria	Top East Coast DJ **STUART BANKS** Eclipse Cambridge - World Party

TOP LONDON DJs

	THE FACE Energy, Raindance	**SLIPMATT** Raindance, Telepathy, Rapido	**TOP BUZZ** Rage, Astoria	

Plus Live PAs

SL II THE NOISE   FROM BELGIUM **T99** PERFORMING ANASTHASIA   **PRODIGY**

More PAs to be confirmed - you won't be disappointed

Plus Alternative Room New Talent - LIME, MASH, DEVIOUS D, PHP, FREESTYLE, DJ R, CRUISE, BUZBY - Booked through Tuffdance 081-530 2409

Tickets are priced £16.50 (No Booking Fee) and are available through: **CREDIT CARD HOTLINE: 0733 60075**

TICKET OUTLETS BIRMINGHAM THE DEPOT 021 643 6045 BOGNOR REGIS ISIS PROMOTIONS 0243 841205 BOURNEMOUTH ORBITAL RECORDS 0202 789445 BRISTOL REPLAY RECORDS 0272 265954 CAMBRIDGE PREMADONNA RECORDS 0223 353325 COLCHESTER WORLD CLASS RECORDS 0206 768979 COVENTRY REVIVE CLOTHING 0203 550750 DERBY B.P.M. RECORDS 0332 382038 EXETER MIGHTY FORCE 0392 433844 FELIXSTOWE DANCE ENERGY 0831 226888 KENT RUSH 0634 580042 LIVERPOOL 3 BEATS 051 709 3355 LUTON SOUL SENSE 0582 23337 MANCHESTER EASTERN BLOC RECORDS 061 228 6432 NOTTINGHAM ARCADE RECORDS 0602 474932 PORTSMOUTH RAZZLES 0705 872877 PETERBOROUGH BOX OFFICE 0733 60075 ROMFORD BOOGIE TIMES 0708 727029 SCOTLAND HOTLINE (ADAM) 031 337 6470 SLOUGH SLOUGH RECORDS 0753 28194 SOUTHEND SOUL MAN RECORDS 0702 335444 SHEFFIELD WARP RECORDS 0742 757585 SWINDON RIVAL RECORDS 0793 542093 SOHO BLACKMARKET RECORDS 071 437 0478 HARROW THE RECORD CENTRE 081 868 8637 ILFORD MUSIC POWER RECORDS 081 478 2080 STREATHAM DANCE FLOOR RECORDS 081 679 5579 ISLINGTON LOUIS MENSWEAR 071 837 0005 ARCHWAY PURE GROOVE RECORDS 071 281 4877 EALING VINYL MANIA RECORDS 081 566 5244 DALSTON NULINE SPORTSWEAR 0836 367479. SEVEN KINGS 0831 284518 SOUTHEND STREETWISE LOUGHTON CAVALIER 081 508 2707.

TICKET AGENTS BRIGHTON MAXINE 0273 27857 BRIXTON ACADEMY BOX OFFICE* CAMBRIDGE MARK 0353 862289 CHERTSEY GERRY 0836 350582/0932 873008 EALING STEVE 0836 349493 EAST LONDON WARREN 081 518 0086 ESSEX GREG 0860 735082 GUILDFORD MARK 0831 242017 GLOUCESTER NICK 0452 615082 HANTS JULIE 0705 261815 HERTS CHRIS 0831 430495 HULL 0482 783666 KENT KYP 0634 575380 KINGSTON UPON THAMES SIMON 081 547 1217 LEICESTER STUART 0860 805021 NEWMARKET STUSSY 0638 741277 NEWCASTLE UPON TYNE NEIL 091 413 2899 NORTH LONDON JEREMY 0860 650661 NORFOLK/SUFFOLK RICHARD 0502 500536/0860 883194 OXFORD ZENA 0865 66911/0831 577474 PORTSMOUTH DARREN 0860 214421 STEVENAGE POPS/LIBERTY 0860 441233/0831 427838 SOUTH LONDON SIMON 0836 557989 STRATFORD SCOTT 081 530 2409 WARWICKSHIRE DANNY 0203 251839 WATFORD BECKY 0923 229276 WEST MIDLANDS JONNO 0831 407004

Coaches are available from:

Oxford - Zena - 0831-577474   Kent - Kyp - 0634-580042   South Coast - Isis - 0243-841205   Leicester - Stuart - 0860-805021

Liverpool - 3 beats - 051-709 3355   Bristol - Replay - 0272-265954   Cambridge - Premadonna - 0223-353325

and buses will be running continuously from Trafalgar Square.

For more information ring - 0831-430495 0831-278637 *To be held at the transformed Brixton Academy - 211 Stockwell Road, London SW9